FORT SUICIDE

Nick L

A World War 3 Technot...   ...ent

Copyright © 2021 Nicholas Ryan

The right of Nicholas Ryan to be identified as the author of this work has been asserted by him in accordance with the copyright, Designs and Patents Act 1988.

This is a work of fiction. Names, characters, places, and incidents either are the product of the author's imagination or are used fictitiously. Any resemblance to actual persons, living or dead, events, or locales is entirely coincidental.

All rights reserved. No part of this publication may be reproduced, stored in or introduced into a retrieval system, or transmitted, in any form, or by any other means (electronic, mechanical, photocopying, recording or otherwise) without the prior written permission of the author. Any person who does any unauthorized act in relation to this publication may be liable to criminal prosecution and civil claims for damages.

Dedication:
As always, this book is dedicated to the one true love of my life; Ebony.
-Nick.

About the Series:

The WW3 novels are a chillingly authentic collection of action-packed combat thrillers that envision a modern war where the world's superpowers battle on land, air and sea using today's military hardware.

Each title is a 50,000-word stand-alone adventure that forms part of an ever-expanding series, with several new titles published every year.

Facebook: https://www.facebook.com/NickRyanWW3
Website: https://www.worldwar3timeline.com

Other titles in the collection:
- 'Charge to Battle'
- 'Enemy in Sight'
- 'Viper Mission'
- 'Fort Suicide'

The Kaliningrad-Lithuania Line

By August the ground war in northern Europe had reached a bloody stalemate.

During the waning days of summer, the Russian Army had been forced out of Warsaw and driven back in disarray to the Poland-Lithuania border where they began preparing defensive lines across the Suwalki Gap to protect their stranglehold on the Baltic States. The Russian fortifications stretched all the way from the southern coast of Kaliningrad to the junction of the Belarusian frontier.

Both armies had been ground down by months of relentless fighting that had soaked the earth with blood and scarred the landscape. Dead men and destroyed vehicles littered fields and highways. Entire cities had been pounded to grey rubble by artillery and missiles.

While the armies were reinforced and re-supplied, millions of displaced refugees streamed west to flee from the fighting. The stench of death and decay hung in the air. Europe cowered in despair, awaiting the next inevitable phase of the war.

Along the Lithuania-Poland border the two exhausted adversaries eyed each other across a narrow four-mile-wide strip of 'no-man's' land. The Russians dug deep trenches to fend off an Allied push into the Baltics and the NATO troops fortified the front line with freshly-arrived units from Britain, France and America.

For several tense days the two forces consolidated their positions. NATO Command knew they must maintain the initiative and continue to pressure the Russian Army that had finally been forced onto the defensive.

The Russians were eager to regain the momentum that had seen their armies sweep victoriously as far west as the outskirts of Berlin. To reclaim their ascendancy, Russian High Command planned a major counter-offensive, redistributing forces and summoning reserves. In secrecy they assembled an assault force of tanks, APCs and soldiers that could punch through the Kaliningrad-Lithuania Line and once again throw open the road to Warsaw.

For a world fatigued by an endless nightmare of atrocities, the last days of summer marked the beginning of a storm of savage fighting that would ultimately place the fate of an entire continent into the hands of a few weary NATO veterans and a smattering of fresh recruits.

The recruits were new to the horrors of war; they anxiously braced themselves for the terrifying trauma of a battle from which many would not survive, and only a very few would emerge as heroes.

In the blood-saturated fields of northern Poland a handful of American infantry standing in the face of the Russian onslaught were put to the ultimate test.

With their backs to the wall and their lives on the line, some men were found wanting… and some discovered a steely resolve that would never allow them to accept surrender at any cost…

Prologue:

It was a plan that would turn the tide of war. An audacious scheme, brilliant in its simplicity and so bold in its vision that it would split the NATO armies in northeastern Poland, and secure Russia's stranglehold on western Europe.

The Russian President personally sanctioned the operation and fourteen Divisions of tanks, troops, and armored personnel carriers were rushed from the Motherland to the Kaliningrad-Lithuania Line. Theater commanders in the Baltics were summoned urgently to Moscow.

In the smoke-filled War Cabinet Room of the National Defense Control Center the Russian President and the Minister of Defense met with military leaders.

The '*Stal'noy kulak* Offensive' was born.

"The setbacks in Poland have been… *unfortunate*," the President of Russia put emphasis on the last word and glowered at the Commander of Western Operational Strategic Command in Northern Europe – a haggard-faced Marshal of the Russian Federation who sat cowered at the far end of the conference table. "We have lost momentum and we must act quickly to seize it back. NATO cannot be allowed to dictate the course of the war. Nor can we allow them time to reinforce. We have bled them dry; now we must strike quickly."

The NDCC was Russia's supreme military command and control base, and the War Cabinet Room was the beating heart of all military operations. The outer walls of the cavernous space were lined with computer workstations and a vast multi-monitor screen that displayed the disposition of every Russian military unit throughout Europe. The Defense Minister got slowly to his feet, double-checking a sheaf of handwritten notes before he scanned the room and cleared his throat.

The months of war had aged the man. His sallow flesh sagged in jaundiced pouches and hung in heavy folds from his jowls. His eyes were red-rimmed; his hair a white unruly shock.

His gaze swung on to the assembled military officers seated at the far end of the table. In a corner of the room a uniformed technician sat poised over a keyboard like a court stenographer. As the Defense Minister spoke, the vast map displayed on the bank of monitors began to change, following the technician's computer-keyed commands.

"We have fourteen fresh divisions newly-arrived in theater," the Defense Minister directed everyone's attention to the display. "Those units are being supplemented with a Division of veteran infantry drawn from our combat troops fighting in Latvia and Estonia."

On the screen the green icons representing the units comprising the 'Iron Fist' were clustered south of the tiny Lithuanian settlement of Reketija, twelve kilometers south west of Kalvarija and close to the Poland-Lithuania border.

"Our strike force is assembled here," the knot of icons flashed for several seconds, "shielded behind a barrier of dense woodlands that stretches like a curtain across the border. NATO has the bulk of its forces guarding the main roads to Suwalki because that is where they anticipate an attack. The rest of their units are strung out along secondary roads. That is the mistake they have made; that is why they will be punished."

The Defense Minister paused for dramatic effect and shook his great unruly mane of hair. He suddenly thrust a finger into the air like a teacher making a point to dim students. "We will strike through the veil of forested land, *north* of the road to Suwalki, taking the enemy by surprise and attacking a vulnerable, poorly-defended stretch of their lines." He stepped back from the table and hung a smug smile of confidence from the corner of his mouth. It was not a reflection of his true feelings. Secretly he despaired that the war was already lost, but such displays of pessimism were a quick route to a firing squad. So, he beamed conviction and put steel into his voice. "The success of the plan depends only on your execution. You have everything you need at your disposal, including the President's personal promise of adequate air cover. When the

'Iron Fist Offensive' begins, the Motherland will require each of you to do your duty. Your performances will be monitored closely."

"When do we launch the attack, Minister?" one officer asked. He was a three-star Colonel general of tanks.

"Seven days from now," the President himself intercepted the question, the tone of his voice daring anyone to object to the timeline. "Another convoy of NATO supply ships is expected to arrive at Bremerhaven three days from now, loaded with troops and equipment from America. We must attack before those relief units can be deployed to the front."

For a long moment the room was stunned into shocked silence.

"Once our tanks have forced a breach in NATO's lines, our troop carriers and infantry will pour through the gap, turning north and south to roll up the Allied flanks and cut them off from reinforcements, leaving the road to Warsaw once again open," the Defense Minister filled the uncomfortable quiet. "Our intelligence reports insist the Allies are stretched thin, and that many of their front-line troops are at half-strength. They are under-supplied and ill-equipped. There will never be a better opportunity to inflict a crushing defeat on them."

"With the greatest respect, Mr. President," a Lieutenant general rose and bobbed his head deferentially. He had a short neck and the oversized muscled shoulders of a weight-lifter. "Seven days does not allow the necessary time to implement your plans. It would be better if we could postpone the action for a few weeks," the speaker ended lamely. For a long moment there was silence. The Lieutenant general swallowed hard and glanced uneasily to the far end of the table.

"Since the time of the Soviet Socialist Republic, we have had plans to cycle from peace to war *in two days*," the Russian President said with menacing calmness. "Those plans called for the mobilization of our entire army against the Fulda Gap. This," the President flung his arm in a wild sweeping gesture at the vast map as his temper began to boil over, "calls for a simple divisional assault against a ten-kilometer wide stretch of enemy line, with the tanks and infantry already assembled. All you need to do is land the first weighted blow against the enemy and they will crumble!" The words became berating, swung like blows, until the officer blushed red. He sank to his seat in subjugation and fearing for his future.

The President glared down the length of the table, his eyes like the twin barrels of a shotgun. "Are there any more questions, or objections?" he planted his bunched fists on the tabletop, the words dripping icy menace.

No one dared speak.

The '*Stal'noy kulak* Offensive' would commence in a week… with the fate of Russia hanging precariously in the balance. The reward for success would be an open road back to Warsaw, an enemy crushed, and a war won.

The consequences of defeat were too terrible to contemplate.

WARSAW
POLAND

Chapter 1:

The embarkation area for deployment forward to the battlefront was a hangar, about a hundred meters long and fifty meters wide, set beside a stretch of abandoned road on the outskirts of Warsaw.

The air overhead was filled Army helicopters, clattering out of the low grey cloud. They circled the LZ like swarming insects on the spinning silver discs of their rotors, whipping up a storm of swirling dust as they flared out to land.

Lieutenant Guy Ponting, newly-arrived from Germany, stood in the yawning entrance of the hangar and let his eyes adjust to the gloom.

The interior was a chaos of soldiers, stores and equipment, including weapons, ammunition and vehicles. The air was thick with the stench of diesel fumes, sweat and cigarette smoke. Heavy metal music blasted from radios, competing with revving engines and the banter of shouting voices. In dark corners, some men tried to sleep. Ponting checked his watch and then wandered into the clamor. A Humvee 2-CT Ambulance with a painted red cross on its side panels loomed out of the cavernous gloom and would have run him down if he had not skittered agilely aside.

A group of soldiers were sitting quietly around a television screen, some slouched on old sofas, others squatted on the concrete floor. CMM was broadcasting footage of the war, reporting live from South Korea. Ponting hovered on the periphery of the group for a few minutes, listening to the reporter. No one paid him any attention.

A sudden incoherent shout from the darkened rear of the hangar cut through the din of noise. Ponting turned his head and narrowed his eyes. Against the far wall, a dozen injured soldiers were laid out on stretchers, their wounds dressed with bandages. Several of the men were hooked up to IV units. Two orderlies and a uniformed doctor wearing surgical masks hovered in the background. One of the wounded men turned his head, and his eyes locked on Ponting. The man pressed two trembling fingers to his lips, mimicking the act of smoking. Ponting hesitated for a moment. Antiseptic tainted the still air. He reached into his uniform pocket and produced a crumpled pack of cigarettes then took a dozen uncertain steps closer. The injured man had a blood-stained bandage wrapped around his forehead, and another wound awkwardly over a gauze pad that covered his left eye. The soldier's pallor was grey as ash. Pain had eroded the sharp edges of his features, misshaping his face and leaving the skin waxen and sagging. There was fear and a kind of madness in his stare, moving like a dark disturbed shadow beneath the surface of a pond.

Ponting crouched beside the man's stretcher and smelled the stench of death. It pricked in his nostrils and coated the back of his throat. He offered the cigarettes to the wounded soldier. Quick as a striking snake the man's hand lashed out and clamped around Ponting's wrist.

"How old are you, Lieutenant?" the soldier rasped.

"Twenty-three," Ponting's eyes flashed with an instant of panic. The man's grip was tight as a vice.

The wounded soldier ran his gaze over Ponting's clean uniform and the innocent features of his face. "You've just arrived. From where? The States?"

"Yes." Ponting could feel himself being pulled off balance by the desperate urgency of the man's clutch. The soldier's one good eye was blood-shot, the creases of his haggard face crusted with dirt and grime.

"You're gonna die," the man pronounced flatly. "The Russians… I've seen things that… that will make you puke. Things so atrocious they're inhuman. This war, Lieutenant – it's gonna chew you up and spit you out."

Ponting swallowed, unsettled. The soldier stared at him with professional pity. Ponting smiled dismissively, but his lips would not hold the shape. He tried to pull away, but the man's hold on his wrist was like a steel clamp. Ponting looked past him; the orderlies were crouched over a nearby man who was choking on his own blood and gasping his last desperate breaths.

"Let me tell you what it's like on the front lines from a Sergeant's perspective," the man's voice was rusty and pain-racked. His lips twisted into a sudden sinister smile. "You think I'm insane. I'm not. This war turns you into an animal…"

Ponting tried to catch the eye of the doctor, his unease rising. The Sergeant's stale breath washed over him as the man sighed.

"This is the story of how an Afghanistan vet and his entire squad became so traumatized by the hell of combat that every one of them threw down their weapons and vowed never to go into action again. After you have heard it, I want you to ask yourself if you're really ready to fight this war." The Sergeant licked dry, cracked lips and his expression turned cruel. His gaze seemed to lose its luster as though he had disappeared into the dark void of a nightmare. Then he began to speak, and his tone turned lulling and hypnotic.

"We were clearing a street on the northern outskirts of a Polish town. There had been heavy fighting in the area. We had the Russians on the run, but they were fighting back as they retreated. Our artillery had pounded the block to rubble, and now we had to go in and clear out the surviving enemy. We called it 'rat-catchin'. It was dirty, dangerous work. We'd been fighting for eight days straight. My men were exhausted, worn down by the strain of constantly being a heartbeat away from death."

He paused and turned his head away, then continued to speak, his tone lowering until the words were barely a whisper.

"A house at the far end of the block was trailing smoke into the sky. The air stank of something sickly-sweet. We cleared the first building and found three Russian soldiers in the ruins. Two of them had been shot in the head. Their faces were unrecognizable. The third man had been shot in the guts. He had crawled across the floor, leaving a wet trail of blood behind him. By the time we arrived his corpse was bloated, the flesh turning purple. A swarm of flies were crawling over his remains, laying eggs in his eye sockets and in his mouth. There was no time to bury the bodies – and fuck 'em; they were only Russians. We moved to the next house and found two more Russians in the front room, both killed by artillery fire. In the rear room of the house, we found a dog and a girl, Lieutenant. The dog had been shot through the head. The girl had been repeatedly raped and then shot. She couldn't have been ten years old. They had tied her to the steel frame of a bed and then used her repeatedly. There was blood all down her legs. After they'd finished with her, they used the barrels of their guns. I guess they shot her when she wouldn't stop screaming." The Sergeant paused to close his eyes, remembering the scene in all its ghastly detail. He started to sob and a single glistening tear ran down his cheek. "It was like that in every building we cleared. In one house we found the remains of an entire family. They had been dragged out into the garden and executed; shot through the head from close range. The two girls had been stripped naked. Their flesh was red from cigarette burns or maybe an iron poker. The Russians had tortured and raped both children before murdering them. One of the girls – a teenager – must have refused to give the Russians what they wanted. They knocked her front teeth out."

The Sergeant drew a deep breath and rolled his head back to face Ponting. "Can you guess what we found in the last house, Lieutenant?"

Ponting licked dry lips and shook his head, his senses reeling, his face blanched white by the horrific tale.

"We found forty Polish residents, all of them dead," the Sergeant's voice cracked. "The Russian soldiers must have killed the men first; herded them onto the sidewalk and mowed them down with their machine guns. There were toddlers too. The Russians crushed their skulls, either with bricks, or maybe by swinging the babies by their ankles against a wall to save ammunition. There was spattered blood everywhere. We found the women in a room at the back of the house. It was a scene of skin-crawling horror. Young, old… it hadn't mattered. The women had all been raped, then shot. The Russians must have torn the clothing off them, then pinned each woman down on the ground while the rest of the soldiers took turns. After each woman had been used, they were discarded, their bodies piled in a heap in the corner and set on fire." The Sergeant's face was beaded with oily sweat and his gaze turned burning black as his voice rose, sobbing and shrill. "That was what we could smell when we started clearing the street. It was the stench of burning flesh."

Suddenly the Sergeant's clamping grip around Ponting's arm loosened, and the young Lieutenant took a staggered step back out of reach. He stared down at the Sergeant, shocked and gasping.

For a moment the Sergeant's expression became lucid. "Do you still think you are ready for war, Lieutenant? Are you ready for the kind of horror I witnessed?" Then he turned his head away.

One of the interns hunched over the Sergeant and felt his wrist for a pulse, then peeled back his eyelid. He jabbed the wounded man's shoulder with a needle and rose wearily to his feet. "Sorry, Lieutenant."

"Was… was what he told me…? Was it true?"

The orderly nodded.

"His head wound? What happened?"

The orderly pulled down the cover of his surgical mask until it hung loose around his neck. The man's face was haggard and creased with lines of fatigue. "Sergeant Yethers attempted to kill himself by putting a bullet in his brain… and he's not the only one who has tried it."

*

The Black Hawk flew nap-of-the-earth, skimming the treetops as it dashed northeast towards the Poland-Lithuania border. Lieutenant Ponting sat strapped into one of the hard troop seats in the cargo bay, the bird's only passenger. At his feet were boxes of supplies and ammunition, lashed to the cabin floor. He stared past the outline of the helicopter's door gunner who stood hunched behind the M-240H machine gun, traversing the barrel in anticipation of enemy fire.

The earth below the racing Black Hawk was horribly chewed by shellfire and brutal fighting. Blackened tree stumps littered a landscape pock-marked with craters brim full of stagnant water. Farmhouses had been razed to the ground and small villages reduced to rubble.

The Black Hawk dipped violently in the air as it swooped to follow the contours of a shallow valley. The door gunner caught Ponting's sudden ashen look of alarm and laughed.

"I hope you didn't eat a big lunch, Lieutenant," the gunner looked over his shoulder. His features were concealed behind a full-faced helmet. "It can get pretty hairy. The Russian SAM stuff in these parts is deadly."

"Have any helicopters been shot down?"

"Hell, yeah. We've lost two birds in the past forty-eight hours," the man's voice crackled loudly in the headphones Ponting wore that were patched in to the helicopter's ICS system. "You're lucky you weren't with us yesterday. We got lit up and fired on by an SA-8. *Jeeeesus!*" the door gunner had a Texan accent and gave a cowboy whoop. "The pilot threw the chopper around, and the automated system built into the bird started pumping out flares as he dived and swerved. The co-pilot damned near shit his pants as the missile flew right past us. Fuck me, it was a wild ride!"

Ponting braced his feet on the floor and clutched at the edge of the seat. The harness he wore bit into his flesh as the Black Hawk plunged down the sky until it seemed to be scraping the ground, then climbed again, the huge turbine engine howling. Icy wind blasted through the open cargo bay doors and filled the interior with dust and debris.

The Black Hawk tilted into a steep right-hand turn and Ponting saw a lake slide by, bordered by a narrow road that led to the small village of Becejty. Then another lake appeared in the distance. The door gunner suddenly became tense. He traversed the machine gun from side to side; the draft through the open door fluttering the sleeves of his uniform. In Ponting's earphones the pilot's calm, matter-of-fact voice announced, "Sixty seconds to LZ."

The Black Hawk skimmed low over the lake, the downdraught from its rotors shattering the mirror-like surface of the water. Through the right-hand open doorway Ponting could see a knoll of elevated ragged ground in the distance. It was in sight for just a moment before the helicopter turned, blocking his view and gaining altitude.

"Thirty seconds to LZ."

The Black Hawk slowed in the air, then reared up on its tail. The whole helicopter seemed to rattle and shudder. Swirling dust filled the cargo bay as the helicopter sank lower, and then settled gently on a flat patch of beaten ground atop the rise, its rotors still beating the air, its turbine whining, impatient to be airborne again.

"End of the line, Lieutenant," the door gunner stepped back from his weapon and unfastened his safety harness. He dropped to his haunches and unhooked the straps that were lashed across the cargo crates. An infantry Sergeant appeared in the open doorway. He had a hard, rugged face, with dark steady eyes. His mouth was a grim slash as he eyed the new Lieutenant and then the few boxes of cargo.

"Jesus, fucking Christ!" the soldier raged, and fixed his steely gaze on the helicopter's gunner. "Where's all the fucking ammo we asked for? And where are the replacement parts for the Humvee?"

The gunner shrugged his shoulders and flipped up the visor of his helmet. His face behind the mask was slick with dripping sweat. "This is all the Battalion sent ya, bud, so this is what you get. You got a problem? Tell someone who gives a fuck. We're just the delivery van."

The crates were unloaded and then Ponting jumped from the loading bay with his rucksack in his hand. His boots landed on clay-baked earth and the sudden heat of the day pressed down on him. He jogged, hunched over, until he was clear of the helicopter's rotors then turned to watch the chopper lift back into the sky, shielding his eyes from the blast of wind-whipped dust.

As soon as the Black Hawk was airborne, the bird tilted to its right, nose down, and dashed away, gaining speed as it headed back towards Warsaw.

"Welcome to COP Bravo Zero-Six, Lieutenant," the Sergeant said stiffly. "Around here, we call the place 'Fort Suicide'. After you've seen your command, you will understand why. I'm your Platoon Sergeant – Sergeant First Class Harley."

Two uniformed men appeared through a break in a barbed wire barricade and hefted the cargo crates to their shoulders under Sergeant Harley's supervision. The men gave the new Lieutenant a contemptuous, dismissive glance but said nothing.

Guy Ponting stood with his hands on his hips and stared northeast towards the Lithuanian border.

He was so nervous he felt physically sick.

BECEJTY
NORTH EASTERN POLAND

Chapter 2:

Combat Outpost Bravo Zero-Six was a squalid hovel atop a scarred patch of high ground with a view all the way to the smoke-smudged Lithuanian border. The outpost's perimeter comprised a concertina barbed wire and wooden post enclosed triangle, each side about fifty meters long. Within the wire wall were three bunkers dug waist-deep into the ground, revetted by sandbags and covered with camouflaged canvas tarpaulins and netting. A separate canvas shroud covered the Platoon's Humvee.

At the very center of the compound stood a watchtower. It was a crude structure made of wooden logs and surrounded by more sandbags. It reminded Ponting of the WW2 prison camp towers he had seen in old movies. The structure stood about fifteen feet high with a corrugated iron roof protecting two men and a heavy machinegun from the elements. From one of the watchtower's upright posts fluttered a faded and weather-tattered American flag.

The ground beneath his boots was beaten, sunbaked earth, and there were gaps in the wire at each point of the triangle that gave access to the LZ and a dirt road that snaked towards the town of Becejty.

The Combat Outpost was located at the north eastern tip of a lake, protected by steep slopes on every side that had been laced with M-18 Claymore mines against an attack. Ponting turned in a slow circle, his eyes appraising the lie of the surrounding land. A narrow tree-lined stream ran away to a patch of marshland, and there were areas of thick forest to the northeast and northwest. Between the two palisades of dense woodlands was a clear, unobstructed view north across a patchwork of churned farm fields to the settlement of Postawelek, about two kilometers away.

Further in the distance, hunched beneath a black scar of smoke, was the village of Szelment, located less than a kilometer from the Lithuanian border. The village stood in the shadow of a wooded grove, and was made indistinct by distance and drifting haze.

A Private came sauntering through a gap in the razor wire. He was unshaven and sloppily dressed. His uniform was sweat stained, his face dark with grime. He stopped chewing gum long enough to ask Ponting, insolently, "Want me to carry your ruck, Lieutenant?"

Ponting nodded. The Private stooped and slung the bag onto his shoulder, then turned on his heel and led the way. As they passed through the barbed wire perimeter, Ponting could feel the stare of hostile eyes assessing him. The Private gave a guided tour of the outpost as he walked. It took less than fifty words.

"Two squad bunkers," the Private said, pointing to the nearest canvas covered shelter. "We rotate because one squad is always on guard duty. We also keep the lookout post constantly manned," he waved an arm at the tower. "The Humvee is under that tarp," he pointed to where the vehicle stood, neglected in a weed-strewn patch of grass. "And here is your command bunker," the Private stopped at the entrance to one of the revetted pits and flicked a sarcastic salute. "Welcome to Hell. We hope you enjoy your stay."

*

Ponting picked up his ruck and carried it down the steps into the gloom of the bunker. The canvas roof, suspended from corner posts, sagged so that in the middle of the floor he could not stand fully upright. He threw his bag onto the narrow bunk and began to unpack the few meager possessions he had brought from the States. The Private lingered in the shadows of the doorway, watching him like a thief. Ponting studied the soldier from the corner of his eye for a moment.

"Who are you?" he asked at last.

"Private Skinner," the man shuffled his feet together and made a half-hearted attempt to straighten his back. "I'm the Platoon RTO, sir." (Radio-telephone operator).

"And the Platoon Sergeant. What's his name again?"

"SFC Harley."

"Yeah. What's he like?"

"Hard as nails, sir. He pretty-much runs things around here," Private Skinner said. "He was in Afghanistan," he added, as if it was all the explanation necessary.

"Where's your former Lieutenant?"

"Gone, sir."

"Gone where?"

"Stateside, sir. He shipped out five days ago."

"And what about the Russians? What have they been up to in the past few days?"

"Nothing we're aware of, Lieutenant."

"No activity? No contact or artillery shelling?" Ponting was surprised.

"No, sir."

Ponting finished unpacking his bag and sighed. "Where is Company HQ?"

"That way," the young Private jerked his thumb. "The Company commander is Captain Gatfield. His headquarters are in the village of Becejty. He's got a platoon with him and the company mortars."

"How often does he inspect our position?"

"Never, sir," Skinner's voice reflected his surprise at the question. "We've never seen or met him."

Ponting kept his features impassive but behind his eyes he was secretly appalled. He went to one wall of the bunker and stared out past the sandbags. Two of the men on sentry duty were reading men's magazines, comparing glossy centerfolds, their weapons discarded. He pressed his lips together with grim resolve. "Pass the word around, Private. Let the men know there will be an inspection in ten minutes. I want everyone paraded."

*

Lieutenant Ponting emerged from the command bunker and walked a slow route around the perimeter of the outpost, checking the coiled razor wire and studying the trench emplacements. The sun was warm on his back and the view north towards the border quiet and serene. A flock of birds swept overhead, flying towards the smoke-smudged horizon. Ponting felt a little of his anxiety and apprehension melt away although his legs carried him stiffly as he completed the circuit.

"This is my command and these men are my responsibility," he thought. "For better or worse, I have to lead them."

Although only one squad was detailed to sentry duty, the men of the Platoon watched him covertly from every vantage point. Even those soldiers who should be sleeping had roused themselves at the sound of the arriving helicopter. They lay in their narrow bunks and watched the new Lieutenant through the netting.

Tom Harley, the Platoon Sergeant, stood with RTO Skinner by the tarpaulin-draped Humvee and watched the solitary figure pick his way through the line of trenches.

"Jesus. He's just a fucking kid," Harley's voice was gruff with scorn. He spat into the long weeds. "Still wet behind the ears and fresh out of Officer Training."

Private Skinner clawed his fingers through his greasy hair. "He asked about you, Sarge. Wanted to know what you were like."

Harley said nothing. Lieutenant Ponting reached the base of the watchtower and looked up, shielding his eyes against the sun. A wooden ladder reached up to the machinegun emplacement. The Lieutenant climbed to the top quickly and stepped onto the shaded platform. The two men manning the weapon shuffled aside so the Lieutenant could survey the scene north.

Harley turned his head to follow the direction of the new Lieutenant's gaze, with the cigarette dangling from the corner of his mouth. On the horizon, beyond the distant village of Szelment, a fresh column of black oily smoke was rising into the afternoon sky.

Ponting suddenly leaned out from the watchtower's platform. "Private Skinner!"

"Sir," Skinner straightened involuntarily and took a pace forward.

"Get the men assembled. Now."

Skinner nodded his head and looked sideways for Sergeant Harley to give the order. The big man dropped the cigarette and crushed the butt beneath his boot, then filled his lungs. His voice boomed across the beaten ground. "The Platoon will assemble beneath the watchtower immediately! Come on you lazy bastards. Move your asses!"

*

The Platoon was made up of forty-two soldiers, divided into three rifle squads, one weapons squad and a six-man headquarters element. Each of the squads was led by a Staff Sergeant. The rifle squads comprised two fire teams and a squad leader while the weapons squad consisted of two machine gun teams, and two close combat missile teams.

Apart from the two men manning the machine gun in the watchtower, everyone in the Platoon formed up in three ragged lines beneath the fluttering flag. Lieutenant Ponting studied the faces of the men in the front rank carefully. He could see the contempt in their expressions; the indolent lethargy in the way they held themselves. They were scruffy, dirty and suspicious. Ponting came to a halt in front of the assembly and clasped his hands behind his back to conceal the fact that they were trembling.

"My name is Lieutenant Ponting," he spoke slowly and clearly with Sergeant Harley at his shoulder. "I've been sent to replace Lieutenant Lewandowski. From what I can see so far there is a lot of work to be done in order to bring this post up to standard, and to turn it into an effective obstacle against an enemy attack. I intend to command the best COP in this man's Army. That means doing things by the book from now on."

There was a murmur of discontent through the ranks and several men exchanged weary, bored glances. Ponting ignored the subtle insolence and was about to continue when from behind him, Sergeant Harley suddenly spoke.

"With respect, Lieutenant," the big man began, his voice tight with restraint. "But the book for this war hasn't been written yet. There is no book for out here. Take a look around. This outpost might not quite be at the ass-end of the world… but you can sure as hell see it from here. We're less than three miles from the enemy and were completely isolated from support."

Ponting bridled at the surly tone. He spun on his heel so the two men stood toe-to-toe. The contrast between the Sergeant and the new Lieutenant was stark. Harley looked old enough to be Guy Ponting's father; his haggard, drawn features etched and scarred by the horrors of combat he had witnessed. He was broad in the shoulder, with muscled forearms and a crop of close-cut greying hair. Lieutenant Ponting smiled thinly, but there was no humor in his eyes.

"I understand the circumstances, Sergeant. Thank you. But I'm also aware of the situation," Ponting's voice was uncompromising. "According to a Battalion intelligence briefing I received before leaving Warsaw, the Russian Army is rumoured to be preparing to mount an offensive, somewhere along the length of the Kaliningrad-Lithuania Line, probably within the next month. If they attack to our front, we'll be overrun. So, effective immediately," he raised his voice, speaking to the Sergeant but addressing the entire Platoon, "we will be conducting a series of aggressive squad-sized patrols, morning, noon and night."

Ponting heard groans of thinly-veiled insolence from the troops and turned back to face them, withering the men to silence with his stare. A couple of the soldiers shuffled their feet in the dirt. From the rear rank several disgruntled men voiced their disapproval.

"The last Lieutenant wanted us to hold our ground."

"We never had to conduct patrols before."

"Quiet!" Sergeant Harley snapped dutifully, and the belligerent protests withered to silence.

Ponting narrowed his eyes and glared at the assembled faces. He could feel his tenuous grip on command trembling in the balance. He was being watched closely by the men who were all studying him with contempt.

"I have made my decision. My orders stand. If the Russians are up to something, I want to know about it well before it happens." He flicked a quick glance over his shoulder and saw smoldering resentment in Tom Harley's eyes. "Dismiss the men, Sergeant."

"Sir," Harley said, then addressed the men. "Dismissed. 'A' Squad will form up at the northeastern gap in the wire at 1300 hours, kitted out and ready to patrol."

Ponting turned away and walked stiffly towards his command bunker. The men he commanded were isolated on the frontlines and facing an overwhelming Russian Army that had already conquered Poland once and might very well make another attempt within days. They were all veterans of the war… and they were scared.

Ponting was a farmer's son from Iowa who had joined the Army before the war out of a sense of duty and a desire to serve his country. He was the first in his family to enlist in the military, and now he saw his noble aspirations for a military career dangling by a thread. He scurried down the steps and into the secluded gloom of the command bunker, the blood pounding in his ears, his whole body hot and sweating.

A sudden sound from the doorway made him spin.

Sergeant Harley stood in the shadows of the entrance, his face hard, his eyes steely. He watched the young Lieutenant for a long time before finally speaking. "Is it true what you said about the Russians?" his voice was gruff and coarse as gravel.

"Are there really rumours that they might be building up to something?"

"Yes," Ponting's voice sounded steady despite his inner dread.

The grizzled veteran Sergeant grunted and nodded his head as though a decision had been made. "Fair enough. If you're playing it straight with me, I'll see to it that you get your three patrols a day… and I'll keep the men in line."

*

'A' Squad, under the command of Staff Sergeant Davin Wagner, assembled by the northeastern breach in the wire perimeter a few minutes before 1300 hours. Platoon Sergeant Harley drew Wagner aside and spoke to him out of earshot of his men.

"The threat of a Russian offensive might be legit," Harley explained his brief conversation with the new Lieutenant. "So, do your job; keep your men alert and bring 'em back alive, understand?"

Wagner nodded. He unfolded a small map he pulled from a pocket, then stared skyward. The afternoon was cloudless and warm.

The two men hunched over the map, and Harley traced a line with his finger towards the dense clump of woods to the northwest. "Recce to the edge of the forest," he said. It was a journey across flat farmland of around a mile, "and then cut north, following the stream as far as the swamp. Then return to base. Understood?"

Wagner nodded. He was anxious. Over his shoulder he could hear his men grumbling as they checked through their equipment. He turned on them, snarling. "Hey! Shut your traps and quit your bitchin'. This is the fucking job, so suck it up!"

Chastened, the men lapsed into surly silence. Harley clapped the Staff Sergeant on the back.

The squad went through the razor wire in single file with Wagner leading the way down the slope. Once they were clear of the Claymore mines, the men fanned out and turned towards the sinking sun at a steady pace. Sergeant Harley climbed the ladder to the watchtower with a pair of binoculars hanging from his neck. He followed the progress of the patrol until it reached the edge of the woods.

*

Staff Sergeant Wagner stepped into the cool margin of the forest and dropped to one knee, pressing his finger to his lips to urge his men to silence. The woods were alive with the raucous chatter of birds. Wagner peeled off his helmet and mopped his brow with his shirt sleeve as the rest of the squad drew close and sank into the long grass.

The men's faces were shiny with sweat. Wagner gave them two minutes to settle in the shade before issuing his orders.

"We're going to push a hundred paces into the woods to conceal our movement and follow the tree line until we reach the stream. Then we'll go north to the edge of the swamp. Understand?"

Heads nodded.

Wagner rose to his feet, standing very still and silent in the shadows, and lifted his gaze once again to the sky. Clouds were building to the south, and as he watched they moved across the horizon piling upon themselves ponderously, heavy with rain.

Then something flashed in the corner of his eye and his head darted to the movement. It was a patch of vivid color, unnatural against the dense green veil of the forest. He felt himself tense.

Two girls appeared from behind a grove of tall fir trees, chatting to each other quietly. They had not seen the soldiers, and they stood, scouring the ground as if searching for something misplaced. One of the girls carried a wicker basket in the crook of her elbow and wore a garland of picked flowers in her hair.

They were teenagers, graceful and slim, dressed in loose peasant skirts of bright color. They dropped to their knees at the foot of a tree and brushed at the fallen blanket of leaves with their hands. One of the girls laughed lightly; a sound like a tinkling crystal bell.

Then – as if warned by some instinct of danger – one of the girls turned and looked over her shoulder. She saw Davin Wagner and started. She pounced to her feet; her face suddenly white with alarm. A hand flew to her mouth. The second girl whirled round. Her eyes grew wide and she began to scream.

"After them!" Sergeant Wagner waved two men forward.

The two girls turned and swirled away like frightened forest animals, the thick braids of their hair bouncing on their backs as they dashed and dodged through the dense undergrowth. They did not get far. Within a few hundred yards the soldiers had hunted the girls down. They brought them back to the margin of the forest. They were sobbing and trembling in fear.

Wagner studied the two girls. They were maybe sixteen or seventeen, their faces slick with tears. They were trembling uncontrollably, cowering away from the soldiers that surrounded them. The Sergeant stared around the circle of troops.

"Anyone speak Polish?"

No one did. But one of the soldiers addressed the girls in German and saw a flash recognition in their expressions.

"Ask them where they're from," Wagner instructed.

The two girls responded with a torrent of words and gestures.

"They say they're from Becejty," the soldier translated. "They say they're sisters."

"And what are they doing so far from the village?"

"They were picking mushrooms," the soldier translated.

Wagner grunted. The basket the girls had been carrying had not been recovered but the story was plausible.

"Ask them if they've seen any Russians in the woods."

"No," came the quick reply, but then one of the girls spoke again, making fluttering and pointing gestures with her hands. The soldier translating the German asked a question and the girl nodded her head. The soldier rubbed the unshaven stubble of his chin.

"This one," he singled out the taller of the two girls, "says she has a friend in Szelment who told her there are Russians in the village, disguised as locals. Her friend was approached on the street by a man who tried to proposition her for sex. When she refused, the stranger became abusive. He dragged her into an alley, but then another man appeared and shouted at the stranger in Russian. The girl claims the man who saved her from being attacked was some kind of Russian officer."

Wagner's expression became alarmed. He told the soldier to make a note of the girls' names and addresses. "And tell them that if they see anything else suspicious, or if they hear more stories from their friend in Szelment about Russian soldiers in the village, they must come to Bravo Zero-Six immediately and report everything they know. Understand?"

The soldier translated. The girls looked to Sergeant Wagner and nodded their heads. He watched them disappear back into the shade of the woods and then drew the rest of the squad around him.

"We're aborting the patrol immediately," he declared. "Double time it back to the fort."

*

Sergeant Harley shouted a warning that the patrol was returning unexpectedly and the troops on sentry duty around the outpost's perimeter became instantly alert. Lieutenant Ponting stood waiting at the gap in the wire as the patrol trudged single file up the slope. The soldiers were sweating under the burden of their bulky equipment. The afternoon had turned humid with the imminent threat of rain.

"What happened?" Ponting frowned.

"We intercepted two local girls from Becejty," Sergeant Wagner snatched off his helmet. "They were in the woods, picking mushrooms when we found them. They told us there are Russian troops in the village of Szelment. They're disguised as locals but doing a bad job of remaining discreet."

Lieutenant Ponting's eyebrows arched in surprise and alarm. He turned his head and stared instinctively towards the distant village. Szelment was just a dark bump on the horizon, obscured by a drifting rain shower.

"The Russians have troops already operating across the border?"

"They might be preparing the way for that attack you said was rumoured," Sergeant Harley clambered down the watchtower ladder to join the conversation, still with the binoculars around his neck.

Ponting frowned, then nodded grimly. "I want all the squad leaders assembled in my office in five minutes."

*

The squad leaders listened in silence to Davin Wagner's report. Lieutenant Ponting waited until the Sergeant had finished detailing his contact with the two Polish villagers and then swept his eyes around the room to gauge the reaction of the other men.

"If the girls are telling the truth, we have a substantial force of Russian troops less than three kilometers from us, on the Allied side of the Polish border," Ponting announced grimly. "I don't believe they're in Szelment on a sightseeing holiday. This information supports the intelligence reports I received in Warsaw, and it suggests an attack against the Allied lines might be imminent. If an assault comes today, or tonight, we'd be overwhelmed in a matter of minutes. So, I want to know what equipment we're lacking. What do we need to fortify our position and to hold off a concerted Russian attack until we are reinforced?"

The squad leaders all spoke at once. Ponting shouted for RTO Skinner. The Private came into the bunker with a notepad in his hand and the stub of a pencil tucked behind his ear.

"We need our night vision gear operating," Davin Wagner said and was supported by a chorus of acrimonious agreement from the other men.

"What's wrong with it?"

"No batteries," Wagner said. "We've got NODs and AN/PAS-13 LWTS gear (light weapon thermal sight) … but we can't get resupplied with the batteries we need. The equipment is nothing but expensive paperweights. It's useless."

"Our best defense is to hold an attack at arm's length," the Sergeant commanding the Platoon weapons squad offered. "So, we'll need more Claymores to mine the slope, as well as the fields in front of our position. And we need more missiles for my Javelins. We have two CLUs and six reloads for each. We'll need at least triple that number of missiles to hold off a wave of Russian armor."

"We need more M249s and more ammunition. The handful of SAWs we have dispersed around the perimeter won't be enough to hold back a frontal infantry assault," another Sergeant insisted.

"We've got to fix the C-wire along the perimeter and add another roll to increase the height of the barrier," Sergeant Harley said. "And we need some armor plate to line the interior of the watchtower walls. That will give the machine gun teams better protection if we come under attack."

Talk swirled around the small table for several more minutes. Lieutenant Ponting listened in silence. The RTO made a note of everything.

"Skinner, I want you to radio that list of equipment to Battalion and tell them we need it all on the next available helicopter. Understand? I also want enough sandbags to protect the front of every entrenchment against a Russian artillery barrage, and I want at least a thousand rounds for the M2 .50cals. And if Battalion can't supply all the Javelin missiles we need, tell them I want a dozen M3 84mm Carl Gustaf recoilless rifles."

"Yes, Lieutenant."

"And I need the tarp stripped off the Humvee. I'm going into Becejty to find Captain Gatfield at Company HQ. He needs to know what's happening in front of our position."

"When?"

"Right now, soldier."

*

A driver steered the Humvee through the gap in the wire, and drove Lieutenant Ponting towards the village of Becejty, with another soldier manning the turret weapon on the Humvee. Ponting was surprised there was little military traffic.

The afternoon overcast was building from the south. Dark clouds lit with flickers of lightning flashed along the horizon. The driver drove fast, and the Humvee swayed on its suspension like a boat on an ocean.

The soldier parked the vehicle on a grassy verge amidst a snarl of Army lorries and Ponting walked into town.

Despite the approaching storm, Becejty was bustling with Allied soldiers. The sidewalks were crowded, the men's voices just a little too voluble and frenetic, as if this day's chance to find drunken pleasure might be their very last.

Ponting saw troops from a dozen different units, and several different nationalities, most of them other ranks, amidst a sprinkling of grimy civilians and farmers. He recognized British and German accents as he wandered through the town, turning into narrow cobblestoned side streets until he passed beneath an arch and found himself in a dead-end alley closed in on either side by the façades of decrepit two-story buildings. The doorways were narrow, and the top story windows shuttered. Overhead, the space between the buildings was strung with clothes washing. The gutters were strewn with broken glass and litter.

The alley was crowded with soldiers, milling around a building with a narrow top-floor balcony, and suspended from it, a lamp glowing red. Standing on the balcony, Ponting could see a young woman with pale skin and long red hair that spilled like lava over her shoulders. She wore just a black lace-trimmed camisole that barely reached to the top of her thighs. She clung to the balcony railing with one hand and waved to the soldiers, provocatively posturing and blowing coquettish kisses.

Ponting was about to turn away when a girl sauntered from the shadows of a nearby door. She wore a grubby peasant skirt and a simple cotton bodice drawn tight around her tender figure.

"I know what you need," the young girl said with a thick Polish accent, brazenly rubbing her body against his like a cat. Her lips were lewdly painted, her eyes old and jaded in the adolescent face.

She told Ponting the price; it was less than the cost of a few loaves of bread.

"How old are you?" Ponting scowled.

The girl had only a basic understanding of English – enough to ply her desperate trade with the Allied troops. "Seventeen," she lied. As she spoke, she led Ponting by the hand towards a dingy building. "Come. There is a place we can go."

Ponting seized her wrist. "Where is your mother? Your father?"

"They are dead," the girl said. "There is just me and my two younger sisters."

The girl looked very thin, and there were smudges under her eyes to show the hardship of her ordeal. "Okay," Ponting relented. "But not in an alley. Come with me. I have a room nearby."

The girl looked surprised. Then she gave Ponting a lascivious smile filled with obscene promise. "And a real bed, yes?"

Ponting nodded. "Yes."

The girl fell in beside Ponting, taking quick running steps on the broken heels of her shoes to keep pace with his purposeful stride. When he reached the archway, he turned left along another cobblestoned street and drew a deep breath. The air seemed fresher now he was clear of the fetid little alley.

The street crested a rise, and on the corner, Ponting found a shabby patisserie. The door hung off its hinges, and the front window was cracked. Inside stood a couple of chairs and tables against one wall, and a counter holding baskets of breadsticks. A middle-aged man wearing a baker's apron lurked in the shadows. He had dark suspicious eyes and the florid complexion of a drunkard. Ponting sat the girl down at the nearest table.

"Food," Ponting called. He went to the counter and leaned across. The baker had a greying van dyke beard. "Do you have eggs? Sausage?"

The vendor glowered at the girl and gave a shrug. Ponting flung a handful of crumpled Euros at the man. The baker's face changed to an expression of delight.

"There is no bed and no room?" the young prostitute pouted at the deception.

"No," Ponting said. "I have paid for food instead. Eat. And then take this," he opened the girl's small hand and filled it with more money. "Use it to take care of your sisters."

The girl looked uncomprehending. "You do not want me for pleasing?" she mangled the sentence but Ponting understood her inference by the crude rehearsed gesture of her hands.

"No," he flashed a rare smile.

The girl's eyes filled with glistening tears, and the tension melted from her shoulders so that Ponting caught a glimpse of the vulnerable child behind the whore's mask. "You are a good man," she sobbed. She leaned across the table to kiss him impulsively. Her lips tasted of her tears. "Thank you." She hid the money in a fold of her long skirt and choked back fresh crying.

"But there is something you can do for me," he said. "I need to find my Headquarters. Have you seen any other American soldiers in the village?"

The girl nodded and pointed. "There are many. They are at the far end of the street, where the road dips and begins to turn."

Ponting nodded his thanks and got up from the table. He went to the counter. "You have been paid well," his voice held a threat and a promise for the vendor. "So, feed her well. If I find out you have cheated me…"

"Yes," the baker bobbed his head and twisted his face into an expression of innocence. "Of course."

Ponting went striding down the cobblestoned street and stopped outside a shop with double glass doors. On the front window *'Sklep Monopolowy'* was painted in yellow lettering next to an image of a wine bottle. Beside it was another sign, this one painted in crude white lettering onto the brick wall.

'US Army D Co HQ'

He went inside.

Chapter 3:

Ponting pushed open the doors and found himself in a large room that had once been the shopfront of a liquor store. Half a dozen men were arguing with a harried Corporal who stood behind a service counter.

"Captain Gatfield is well aware of the defensive measures necessary to fortify the village from Russian attack," the Corporal insisted. "And as soon as he signs the necessary orders, the work will commence."

"Listen bud," a burly short-tempered supply Sergeant leaned across the counter, his face swollen with frustration. "I've got a dozen lorries parked on the outskirts of this damned village and they're all loaded up with wire, ammunition and equipment. I need to know where to unload."

"I can't tell you that," the Corporal said. "That's up to Captain Gatfield to decide."

"Then find Captain Gatfield!" the supply Sergeant bellowed. His boots and uniform were spattered with mud and his face was grey and haggard with fatigue. He looked like he had just come off the front line. "Where is the XO?"

"Lieutenant Manning is in the village inspecting the perimeter. Go and look for him."

Ponting waited until the other soldiers had all left and he was alone. The Corporal looked up from a computer screen at the new face and sighed.

"Captain Gatfield is not here," he said, and then belatedly added, "sir."

"Where is he?"

"In meetings."

"Then you had better interrupt him, immediately," Ponting said. "I'm Lieutenant Ponting. I've just flow from Warsaw to take command of Bravo Zero-Six. I have urgent intelligence for the Captain; information about Russian troops moving covertly across the Lithuanian border into Poland."

"But the Captain –"

"And every minute you stall," Ponting menaced, "increases the threat. This is urgent intelligence that must be presented to the Captain as soon as possible."

The Corporal stared defiantly for a long moment and then blinked. "I have strict instructions directly from the Captain that he is not to be disturbed…"

"This is urgent intelligence."

The Corporal drew a deep breath and finally capitulated. "He's not here."

"Then where is he?"

"Several German high-ranking officers are visiting Becejty. They're on an inspection tour of their Army's troop positions throughout northern Poland. They commandeered a farmhouse at the far end of the village. Captain Gatfield was invited to attend a liaison briefing and an intelligence update. That's where he is."

*

The farmhouse stood on the ridgeline of a gentle rise overlooking a lush green valley to the west of Becejty. Ponting's driver parked the Humvee in front of the sprawling old stone building amidst a traffic jam of other vehicles.

The front door of the farmhouse was wide open. From somewhere inside the building came a faint roar of raucous laughter. Ponting stepped into the entry hall and looked about impatiently. The interior was cool and gloomy, lit by dozens of flickering candles. The farmhouse smelled of stale alcohol, perfume and cigarette smoke.

Ponting stepped along the hallway, following the sounds of laughter.

A door at the far end of the hall opened and a teenage girl appeared. She was naked but for a pair of sheer black satin panties.

"You're late to the party," she purred with a thick accent. She glided across the room towards him and draped her arms around his neck. He felt the hot bare flesh of her press against his chest. "Do you want to find a room? The Germans have paid for everything."

Ponting recoiled and untangled himself from the girl. She tottered to keep her balance and pouted at him, frowning.

"I'm looking for Captain Gatfield. He's an American officer. Have you seen him?"

The girl lost interest and her eyes became hooded. She tossed her head and pointed to a door. "Everyone is in there," she simpered.

Ponting pushed open the door and stepped on an empty wine bottle. The sudden sound of smashing glass turned every head in the room.

There were a dozen uniformed officers standing, drinking and laughing coarsely, while scantily clad young girls flitted around the room like butterflies. In a darkened corner a young woman was naked on her knees before a tall grey-haired German Colonel. The officer turned, scowling.

"Who are you?" he demanded, his tone brusque and imperious.

"Lieutenant Ponting," Ponting stiffened. "I have urgent intelligence for Captain Gatfield, US Army."

"Ponting? Christ man, what are you doing here?" an American officer emerged from the crowd. He was holding a tumbler of scotch, the rim smeared with a woman's pink lipstick. He was a man in his late thirties, overweight and round in the shoulder. His expression was a mixture of astonishment and acute embarrassment.

"I have urgent intelligence, sir. It's about the Russians on the border."

"For God's sake, man," Gatfield pulled at Ponting's arm and steered him back into the hallway, flushing with sudden irritation. "Couldn't this wait until tomorrow?"

"No, sir," Ponting stood his ground.

"Christ!" Captain Gatfield looked closely at the young Lieutenant, and it was clear he was trying to place the man. "Where did you come from?"

"I'm the replacement Lieutenant at Bravo Zero-Six, sir. I flew in from Warsaw today."

Gatfield narrowed his eyes and sighed indulgently. "Very well, Ponting. Make your damn report."

Ponting repeated the details of the midday patrol's encounter in the woods with the two village girls. "If their information is correct, it means that combat elements of the Russian army are already in Szelment, most likely preparing the way for a concerted armored assault that could come at any moment. At the very least, Battalion HQ must be notified, and Becejty fortified. My outpost desperately needs equipment and ammunition."

"One day on the battlefront and you're already presuming to tell me my duty, Lieutenant?" Gatfield arched his eyebrow in a pantomime of haughty arrogance, then withered Ponting with his glare.

Ponting shook his head. "Sir, I'm telling you what I need to defend my position against a Russian attack."

"And I've noted your request," Gatfield became terse with impatience. He herded Ponting back down the hallway, through the front door and out onto the porch. "You're dismissed, Lieutenant."

*

When Guy Ponting returned to Fort Suicide, he was grim-faced and seething with frustration. It was late afternoon in northern Poland, the sun slowly sinking towards the horizon behind a smear of smoke. The afternoon storm that had threatened a torrential downpour had slid harmlessly over the rim of the southern skyline, missing the region around Becejty.

Ponting's driver parked the Humvee within the outpost's wire perimeter. Sergeant Harley approached. He had his M4 carbine slung over his shoulder and was applying camouflage paint to his face with broad swipes of his thumb.

"I take it that your meeting with Captain Gatfield did not go well," the Sergeant said with a tone of weary resignation.

"No," Ponting confided, keeping his voice low and out of earshot of the rest of the Platoon. "He said he would note my request for more ammunition and equipment."

"You told him about the two Polish villagers and what they reported?"

"Yes. It made no difference."

Harley sighed and turned to stare north into the distance. He finished camouflaging his face and wiped his paint-stained fingers on his uniform. The village of Szelment had become smudged into the skyline by the fast-approaching night. All that could be seen of the settlement were a few pale pinpricks of light.

"If the Russians attack tonight…" Sergeant Harley didn't need to finish the sentence. In his mind he had the sudden chilling vision of a sky lit up by arcing flares and a wall of enemy tanks advancing behind a storm of artillery.

"Yes," Lieutenant Ponting agreed, then roused himself from the mire of his fatalistic thoughts and glanced over his shoulder. The men of 'B' squad were assembling at the breach in the wire. "You're leading the night patrol?"

"Yes," the Platoon Sergeant answered. "I'll head northwest to the woods and then follow the course of the stream until I reach the marsh."

"Good," Ponting suddenly pushed himself away from the Humvee, a decision made. "I'll be patrolling with you."

"Sir?"

"I'm joining the patrol, Sergeant. It's the best way for me to learn the terrain."

"Are you sure that's a good idea, sir?"

"Yes," Ponting's mind was made up. "But it will be your patrol; you know the lay of the land. I'll be joining the column."

*

They left Fort Suicide just as the sun dipped below the rim of the horizon. The sky was still a riot of molten purple hues as the patrol went single file down the slope and into the long grass of the open fields. Clouds had returned with the onset of dusk, hanging low over the treetops and trapping the lingering warmth of the day.

Sergeant Harley led, with Lieutenant Ponting in the middle of the line.

By the time they reached the fringe of the woods to the northwest of the COP, the night was finally on them and it had begun to rain; a drizzling mist that turned the darkness into veils of pearlescent gloom.

They skirted the edge of the woods, the ground crunching beneath their feet, the long grass swishing around their boots as they stepped.

Guy Ponting sensed, rather than saw the men around him. The darkness was absolute. The equipment they carried squeaked and rustled. Once a man near the front of the line coughed and Sergeant Harley turned on him savagely.

They reached the northern edge of the forest. A break in the overcast suddenly exposed them to pale starlight. Sergeant Harley went down on one knee in the tall grass and signaled the men behind him to freeze.

The rain stopped abruptly.

The patrol waited, stationery and alert for sixty seconds, before Sergeant Harley rose cautiously to his feet and resumed his advance. The gradient beneath the men's feet began to rise in a gentle incline.

The eerie quiet after the rain startled Lieutenant Ponting. In the silence he could hear the rasping breath of the soldier behind him and the small sounds of each man's gasping effort. The brush of the grass around their legs sounded jarringly loud. From the forest trees came the haunting hoot of an owl and then the dark swish of beating wings.

All of the Lieutenant's senses became heightened to compensate for the debilitating darkness. He could smell the earthy mustiness of the ground, the rotting vegetation, and the musky sweat of the men around him. He could feel the soft breath of a breeze on his cheek, and he could sense the men's rising anxiety as they finally reached the bank of the stream.

The water was black and the weed-grown banks a muddy bog. Insects buzzed noisily in the darkness. The course of the stream meandered away towards the north west, showing as a darker shadow on the landscape. Sergeant Harley called a halt to the patrol and went down on his knee behind the shelter of a dense grove of waist-high bushes. Lieutenant Ponting crept forward. The Sergeant pressed his mouth close and whispered.

"From here we follow the bank of the stream," he indicated the shadow of ground that snaked away into the distance. "The marsh is about a click away."

"No," the Lieutenant shook his head abruptly. "I want you to lead the patrol towards Szelment. There is an elongated grove of forest about a mile outside of the village. Take us there."

"But Lieutenant –"

"That's an order, Sergeant Harley," Ponting hissed. "I'm changing the plan. If the Russians are massing troops and equipment around Szelment, I want to know about it."

Sergeant Harley gave a curt nod and signaled the men to their feet. Ahead of them the clouds that had blanketed the horizon began to lift, revealing Szelment silhouetted on the skyline, the village marked by pinpricks of pale, far-away light.

"Move out," Sergeant Harley passed the word down the line. "We're moving out. Keep in formation and don't make a fucking sound if you want to stay alive."

*

The squad moved north, serpentining in single file through the long grass, and across fields that had long ago been under the plough. The ground was corrugated and treacherous, rising and falling in gentle undulations as it followed the contours of the land.

The men moved with the weight of rising tension on them, measuring each step, moving like wraiths in the dark.

The dense silhouette of the forest loomed ahead. To their right and in the middle distance, the village of Szelment took on vague shape. Ponting could see the spire of a church and the gleam of an iron roof reflecting starlight. There were lights burning in the village; small square patches of pale yellow glow in an otherwise black and forbidding night.

They reached the rim of a shallow depression and Sergeant Harley signaled for the patrol to stop. Ahead of them lay a reed-choked swamp that barred their path. It had not been marked on the map. Sergeant Harley hesitated. A detour would take them too close to the village. Lieutenant Ponting reached the head of the column.

"We've got no other choice," he said. "We have to go through it."

Sergeant Harley led the men down the embankment and into the marshy ground. Mud and slime reached to their knees, then rose as high as their waists. The men waded through the molasses that sucked and gurgled around their bodies as they passed. The reeds grew higher than their heads and they lost sight of the lights of the village. They came out of the stinking ooze coated in filth, arms and legs aching and numb from the exertion.

They rested for five minutes. A sliver of moon made a brief appearance and then disappeared back behind clouds. But the fleeting moments of light were enough for Ponting and the Sergeant to get their bearings. Ponting crouched low in the grass and studied the village of Szelment through binoculars. Little could be seen in the darkness, but the lights in the village windows glowed brightly enough for him to detect vague movement. There were vehicles on the streets and shifting shadows moving past the windows.

It was another fifteen minutes of slow, painstaking progress before the patrol finally reached the shadowed margin of the grove. By then every man in the squad was physically and mentally exhausted. They slumped down in the dark tangle of undergrowth while, once again, Lieutenant Ponting crept forward to study the distant village through binoculars.

He was close enough now to identify the blurred shapes of several buildings. He studied each one closely and focused the powerful magnifying lenses on every lit window. On the gentle breeze, he thought he detected the rumble of heavy engines. He cocked his ear to the side and concentrated his mind. The sound came in undulating indistinct waves, too muffled by distance to be identified.

He was about to wriggle back into the deep shadow of the forest when a hand seized his arm. He spun his head round. Sergeant Harley's eyes and white teeth showed through the makeup of his camouflage paint. He pressed a finger to his lip and whispered.

"We're not alone," the Sergeant's words screwed a knot of tension tight in Ponting's guts. "I heard Russian voices away to our left, coming from somewhere inside the woods."

Ponting, Harley and two others ghosted forward, following the sound of the voices, while the rest of the patrol quietly found cover to fend off an attack. Sergeant Harley could smell the faint scent of cigarette smoke. He sniffed the air like a bloodhound and changed direction, pushing deeper into the darkness of the forest. Ponting and the others followed his footsteps. The Lieutenant barked his shin on a jagged knot of wood and grimaced in pain.

Finally, the Sergeant sank down to his knees and pulled Ponting to the ground beside him.

"They're directly to our front, maybe twenty paces," Sergeant Harley said, indicating the direction with his open hand. "I can hear them. We should turn back, sir," he spoke in a breathy whisper.

"No," Ponting became stubborn. "This confirms the Russians are massing troops. I need to know what we're facing. How many men do you hear?"

"Two voices," Sergeant Harley shrugged. "But there might be more."

"An outpost? Scouts?"

"Maybe."

Ponting fell into silent calculating thought for a moment. "We'll have to chance it," The Lieutenant decided. "We have to take them out – quietly."

"Sir, that is a damned foolish idea," Sergeant Harley hissed. "We don't know what we're up against. There could be a whole fucking Battalion in this forest."

"There's only one way to find out."

Before the Sergeant could protest further, Ponting rose impetuously and went forward. He reached a fallen log and peered ahead into the blackness. He thought he detected the silhouettes of two figures, standing close together with their backs against a tree trunk. Beside him Sergeant Harley fumed in bitter agitation.

Ponting held up two fingers. Sergeant Harley nodded. Now their eyes were adjusted to the blackness, vague shapes could be determined. All four US soldiers drew knives and stalked forward like ghosts.

The two Russian soldiers manning the outpost were taken by complete surprise. Sergeant Harley sprang from the bushes and clamped his hand over the mouth of the closest enemy soldier, arching the man's back like a bow and pulling him off balance. The Russian flailed his arms and staggered. Harley felt the Russian's weight press back against him. He raised the knife and it glinted wickedly in the night. The Russian saw his death approaching and tried to scream but the Sergeant's grip over his mouth was vice-like. The blade of the dagger plunged deep into the Russian's heart. Warm blood gushed over Harley's hand. The enemy soldier struggled for another frantic moment and then went suddenly limp and lifeless. Harley lowered the dead body to the ground and whirled round.

The second Russian soldier tried to flee into the night. Lieutenant Ponting crash-tackled the man to the ground. The two other American soldiers fell upon the flailing soldier like frenzied fiends, plunging their knives into his chest. The Russian's legs kicked and he made a gurgling, choking sound. Lieutenant Ponting clamped his hands tight around the Russian's throat and strangled the life from him.

Ponting got to his feet, his chest heaving like a bellows for breath. He had just killed his first man. He had imagined this moment a hundred times. He had expected to feel a sense of primal elation or triumph. Instead, he felt a deep empty despair. He looked down at his fingers and they were shaking.

"Hide the bodies," he ordered the two soldiers who still held their blood-coated knives in their hands. His voice, despite the moment, sounded cold and remote. "Sergeant Harley. Bring the rest of the squad forward."

Harley looked disbelieving. "You want to keep going, Lieutenant?"

"Yes. I need to know what the Russians have hidden in this forest, and I'm not returning to base until I get the answers."

"But, sir. If the Russians we killed are discovered –"

"My mind is made up, Sergeant," Ponting's voice turned harsh. "Bring the rest of the squad forward. That's an order."

*

The squad moved deeper into the forest with Lieutenant Ponting taking point position. They stumbled across a narrow trail and the going became easier. It was a worn path through the tall trees, wide enough for two men. The route meandered into the darkness, past rocky outcrops and dense palisades of shrubs where enemy sentries could have been hidden. Ponting's training told him that such dangerous places should have been cautiously reconnoitered, but he had a fatalistic, reckless determination to justify his decision to continue the patrol. Maybe, he fretted, he should have heeded Sergeant Harley's advice and turned back to Fort Suicide. The odds, and time were heavily against him. It was possible that the Russians had already discovered their two dead comrades and were, at this moment, scouring the forest searching for their killers. It was possible, too, that the notion the Russians were secretly massing armor and equipment in the forest was a fantasy of the Allied intelligence community's imagination, and that in the end, the reward for his impetuous decision would be nothing but sore feet and a night of lost sleep.

Almost an hour into the march they reached a gentle rise of densely forested ground. Ponting rested the men on either side of the trail while he crawled to the crest with Sergeant Harley at his side. There was a strange pale light in the sky; a reflected glow against the belly of the clouds. Ponting held his breath and in the sudden crushing stillness heard noise.

It was the *'clank'* of something metallic, followed by a low muttered curse. Ponting and Harley exchanged glances. Moving with infinite painstaking stealth they wormed their way to the lip of the ridge and peered cautiously into the darkened depression before them.

"Good God," Sergeant Harley breathed, for he could suddenly see the reason for the glow against the clouds. Dozens of Russian tanks and armored personnel carriers were scattered through the forest. The lights were hooded arc lamps, being used by Russian maintenance crews to prepare the vehicles for battle. As the two Americans watched in rising horror, a handful of enemy soldiers began loading sabot rounds through the turret of one of the tanks, working and cursing quietly under their breath in the awkward conditions.

Ponting felt a lift of relief and, at the same time, a premonition of imminent disaster. He began counting the tanks. The closest vehicles were T-90s but there were others, further away and cloaked in darkness, that he could not identify for certain. The APCs were Russian BMP-2s. He pulled the binoculars to his eyes and swept the depths of the forest. Shadows moved in the night, and beyond the reach of the magnifying lenses he heard an engine cough to life. It was left idling for a few seconds and then was shut down.

"I count twenty-one MBTs and sixteen APCs, plus supply vehicles," he muttered in a hoarse whisper. Harley nodded. The force was not enough to constitute a major Russian offensive, but it was a formidable threat and, likely, there were many more tanks and APCs hidden in the night beyond sight.

Ponting lifted the glasses again and searched for another thirty seconds. An arc light flashed across the crest, forcing both men to duck below the rise. The light swept over the ridge and then was gone again.

"We have to get back to the fort and contact Battalion," Ponting said. "The Russians have tanks and equipment already across the border and are building up for a major assault – and we're the only ones who know about it."

They wriggled back off the crest and rose quietly to their feet. Sergeant Harley gathered the squad about him. "We're getting out of here and we're going fast," there was strain and urgency in his hushed voice. "Don't make a fuckin' sound and don't stop to smell the flowers."

They went quickly, following the trail, with Ponting leading the patrol and Sergeant Harley at the tail of the column, protecting the vulnerable rear. Lieutenant Ponting reached the point where they had intercepted the worn path when suddenly a shot rang out in the darkness from somewhere to their front. Ponting threw himself sideways into a tangle of bushes just as the night erupted into juddering flickers of muzzle flash and a deafening roar of gunfire. The fury of the fusillade echoed through the forest and lit up the darkness. In the aftermath of the initial outpouring of fire one of the Americans lay dead on the ground, a bullet in his neck and his blood soaking into the dirt.

"Contact front! Engage!" Sergeant Harley shouted from the rear of the column, cutting laterally through the dark tangle of forest. His instinct told him they had stumbled on a Russian unit patrolling through the woods. Harley knew the squad could not afford to become pinned down by a prolonged firefight. The enemy had to be rooted out before reinforcements arrived.

He charged through the undergrowth, keeping low, moving in a wide circle. He judged the position of the Russians by the flash of their gunfire and kept plunging through the undergrowth until he was sure he had encircled the Russian patrol's flank. Then, more stealthily, he closed on the pathway from out of the forest, creeping towards the flashing lights of gunfire. The American patrol were firing back at the Russians, blazing away to suppress the enemy's fire. Sergeant Harley crept to within twenty meters of the path and lobbed a grenade.

"Frag out!"

The sudden thunderous explosion sounded like the *'crump!'* of an artillery shell in the enclosed space of the forest trail. For a split-second a violent white flash lit the night and then the ground around the Russians heaved up, and the air filled with killing fragments. In the stunned eerie silence that followed he could hear wounded Russians screaming and groaning. The Americans sprang to their feet and dashed forward, firing as they closed on the enemy soldiers.

A Russian with his hands covering his face and blood streaming through his fingers staggered in a blind circle and then fell to his knees, screaming in agony. The blast of the grenade had shredded his uniform to tatters and ripped open his chest. Sergeant Harley shot the man in the back of the head.

He turned at the waist and saw two more Russians on the verge of the path, one of them clutching at his thigh, but before he could aim his M4, fire from the advancing squad killed them, knocking both men down and shredding the surrounding foliage to tatters.

Lieutenant Ponting lead the charge, hurdling a dead Russian body, an incoherent cry of fear and exultation in the back of his throat. He stumbled on a tangle of tree roots and fell into a puddle of warm spattered blood, just as a burst of enemy gunfire from out of the darkness blazed inches from his head, so close that he could feel the wind of its passage against his face. Sergeant Harley seized the Lieutenant by the scruff of his collar and heaved Ponting to his feet.

There were two surviving Russians, shooting from a shallow depression. It was panic fire, blazed across the path. A stray bullet struck Lieutenant Ponting in the shoulder and threw him back down onto the ground, flat on his back.

"Man down! Man down!" Sergeant Harley shouted. He dropped to his knee in front of the wounded Lieutenant to shield his body and returned fire on the Russian position. The soldier who had been standing next to Harley threw a grenade. The explosion was shocking, the flash searingly bright against the darkness. The two enemy soldiers were hurled into the air by the force of the explosion, their bodies cartwheeling and limbs flailing. They were dead before they hit the ground.

"Fuck!" Sergeant Harley threw down his weapon and reached into the pockets of his uniform for a field dressing. He thrust it into the bullet hole in Ponting's shoulder. Bright warm blood soaked the haemostatic gauze and ran thick across his fingers. He felt the Lieutenant's cheek; the flesh was cold and clammy. Ponting's eyes stared sightlessly up into the dark sky, his mouth hanging slack and his breathing shallow. Harley grimaced and cursed bitterly under his breath.

"You and you!" he stabbed his bloody fingers at two nearby soldiers. "Take turns carrying the Lieutenant. The rest of you, form up and move out. We're double-timing it back to the fort."

*

The squad reached the fringe of the forest and struck southeast towards the silhouetted rise of the Combat Outpost, far away on the night's skyline. Free from the claustrophobic confines of the dense forest, the air was cool and the night brighter so that each man showed clearly beneath the soft starlight.

Sergeant Harley called a brief halt. The men were grim-faced and filthy with dirt and sweat. They stared at the Sergeant through red-rimmed eyes and listened in sullen silence.

"Tonks," he singled out a broad-shouldered squad member with a flat face and a buzz-cut of sandy hair. "You're staying with me. The rest of you are to push on to the fort. Get the

Lieutenant to safety and whistle-in a medivac chopper. Tonks and I will be the rearguard. If the Russians mount a pursuit, we'll hold them off for as long as we can." He reached into Lieutenant Ponting's pocket for a notebook and pencil and scratched a hasty message noting the Russian equipment the patrol had discovered in the forest. Lieutenant Ponting was slung over a man's shoulder in a fireman's lift, the soldier's uniform soaked with the wounded officer's blood. "If the Lieutenant doesn't make it, tell the RTO to get this message to Battalion. It's urgent."

The squad moved off, wading through the long grass in single file. Harley and Private Tonks sank down into the grass behind a cluster of boulders to wait.

Russian pursuers emerged from the woods fifteen minutes later; a Platoon of men moving fast across the open field. Their shapes were grotesque apparitions in the starlit night – dark hulking silhouettes, heavy with equipment. They fanned out in a line and advanced.

"Let them come closer," Sergeant Harley whispered to Tonks. The Russians were moving with purpose and precision, keeping their spacing, following the waved instructions of the Lieutenant who led them. Harley swung his M4 until the Russian officer was in his sights and inhaled a deep, settling breath.

"Fire!"

The sudden whipcrack of automatic fire flung the Russian officer down in the long grass and threw three more enemy soldiers to the ground screaming.

"Ataka! Ataka!" The Russian word of command carried clear across the night. The Russians at either end of the line dropped to their knees and began giving covering fire, blazing away into the night in an attempt to suppress the Americans and allow the men in the middle of the line to charge their position. Sergeant Harley stubbornly refused to duck for cover and instead fired again, picking off two Russians as they drew close. The first man cried out in agony as the bullets socked meatily into his chest, punching him backwards. The second

man went down in spatter of blood, buckling at the knees and seeming to hang suspended for a moment before he collapsed.

Private Tonks lobbed a grenade at the advancing enemy. The explosive arced high into the air but fell short of the advancing Russians. The brilliant flash of its detonation shook the night and painted the enemy in a brief flare of stark, dazzling light.

Sergeant Harley peered through the smoke to find a nearby target. He saw a Russian soldier off to his left, trying to outflank their position. He aimed and the M4 kicked against his shoulder as he fired.

Then the darkness was lit by the trajectory of a white flare that hung high in the sky overhead and turned the night into day. It had been launched from Fort Suicide. Harley and Tonks seized their opportunity. They fired one last time, then turned and scrambled away through the long grass. The Russians were forced to go to ground, caught horribly exposed in the open. By the time the flare had finally burned out and the night had closed back down over the fields, the two Americans were long gone.

When Sergeant Harley and Private Tonks reached the barbed wire perimeter of Fort Suicide, the compound was on high alert. Lieutenant Ponting lay on a stretcher on the edge of the LZ. Nearby a column of red billowing smoke trailed into the night sky.

"A medivac Black Hawk is on its way from Warsaw," RTO Skinner explained to the Sergeant.

Harley grunted. He ordered another flare fired into the night, although he doubted the Russian pursuers would dare come within automatic weapons range of the outpost. Then he shrugged off the bulky weight of his equipment and strode to the far side of the LZ. The Platoon's medic was on his knees beside the Lieutenant's stretcher rigging an IV line. Ponting's shoulder wound had been dressed and bandaged. The Lieutenant looked ashen, his eyes glazed and unfocussed.

"Is he gonna make it?" Harley asked.

"Yeah. It looks worse than it is," the medic sounded bored. "I've given him a blood expander to counteract the blood loss."

The helicopter arrived out of the night, the sound of its beating rotors announcing its appearance long before the dark bulk of its shape could be seen. The pilot set the bird down on the LZ. Harley and the medic carried the stretcher to the open cargo bay door. The Black Hawk had been on the ground for less than fifteen seconds before it lifted off again, sliding across the night sky as it turned and headed back towards Warsaw.

Chapter 4:

Guy Ponting woke up in an Army field hospital on the western outskirts of Warsaw with an IV drip line dangling from his arm and a pretty blonde nurse leaning over his bed. The nurse's brow was furrowed as she studied Ponting's chart, then reached for his wrist to take his pulse.

"What time is it?" Ponting's head felt stuffed with wool, and his words came out slightly slurred.

The nurse looked close to exhaustion. There were fine lines of fatigue beneath her eyes and at the corners of her mouth. "It's afternoon," she said. "You've been here since late last night."

Ponting tried to sit up in the bed. "I need to make a report. I have important information that must reach my Battalion HQ."

He worked manfully at a computer terminal until the early evening, uploaded his report, and then slept for twelve hours. In the morning he felt better. The bullet wound was high up on his left shoulder. The nurse strapped his arm in a sling and he spent the rest of the morning prowling the hospital ward, restless and impatient. At midday two officers arrived at the field hospital.

"Lieutenant Ponting, I am Major Wayland Young, Battalion S2, and this is Captain Anson from Army Intelligence. We're here to discuss the report you filed regarding a squad contact and subsequent firefight with Russian troops in the vicinity of Szelment."

The Battalion Major who made the introductions was an overweight man in his forties with a round fleshy face, grey hair and sharp, intelligent eyes. The Captain from Army Intelligence was ten years younger and fifty pounds lighter. Captain Anson had the mannerisms of an undertaker; a dour, humorless face and a troubled expression.

"What else do you want to know?" Ponting propped himself against a wall.

Major Young began the questioning. Captain Anson retrieved a notebook from his pocket and transcribed everything Ponting said. The Major ran his fingers across his cheeks like he was trying to pull his face into a friendly smile before he asked his first question.

"Tell us again exactly what Russian vehicles you claim you saw in the forest northeast of the village."

"I saw sixteen Russian BMP-2 troop carriers and twenty-one main battle tanks. The majority of those tanks were T-90s. Some I could not clearly identify. They might have been T-90s or maybe T-72s."

"So, you're not sure."

"Not sure of what?"

"Not sure exactly what you saw."

"I am sure of what I saw," Ponting snapped. "And Sergeant Harley can verify the contents of my statement. He was with me."

"Yes," The Major acknowledged. "We've spoken to Platoon Sergeant Harley. He said it was very dark. He also said he counseled you to fall back to Combat Outpost Bravo Zero-Six after an initial contact with the enemy – a recommendation you ignored."

"That is correct," Ponting conceded. "I chose to continue the patrol because my instincts told me there was a chance the enemy had a substantial force concealed in the forest. I felt it was important to prolong the reconnaissance."

"So, is it possible you felt you *had* to find some trace of the enemy?" the Major feigned delicacy. "Otherwise, you would have looked foolish in the eyes of your men, right?"

"What are you suggesting?" tension came into Ponting's expression. This meeting wasn't an interview, it was an interrogation.

"Nothing," the Battalion Major shrugged and suddenly made himself appear innocent. "I'm simply trying to consider all the possibilities."

"Are you suggesting I fabricated the report in order to justify the decision to continue the patrol after we had eliminated the two Russian sentries?"

"Is it possible?"

"No."

Major Young nodded his head like a sage defense attorney and changed tack. "How long had you been at the battlefront before you were wounded in action, Lieutenant?"

"One day."

"Less than that, in fact. Closer to twelve hours, correct?"

Ponting nodded.

"Well, is it possible your inexperience of combat situations might somehow have colored your description of the Russian force you claim to have seen in the dark forest, in the middle of the night?"

"No," Ponting said flatly. He gave the Major a venomous glare of defiance and his tone became hostile. "I know what I saw. It's all in my report."

"Very well," Major Young smiled thinly and ended the interview with an abrupt shrug of his shoulders. "Thank you for your time, Lieutenant."

The two officers made to leave. Ponting called after them. "When can I get out of here? I want to return to my Platoon."

"Three days," Captain Anson said.

"My post needs ammunition and equipment… I listed everything in my report."

"Yes. Your request has been noted. Good day, Lieutenant."

*

Major Young remained tight-lipped until the two officers had moved well beyond the neat ranks of hospital buildings and were striding up a rise of muddy grass to where their Humvee was parked. On the far side of the clearing a Black Hawk was landing, kicking up a whirlwind of dust. The Major watched the chopper settle on the ground and offload two stretcher-bound soldiers before he finally voiced his thoughts.

"I think Lieutenant Ponting believes he saw what he claims," the Major said.

Captain Anson bit his lip. "But that doesn't mean you believe he actually saw anything at all. You're saying you don't think he's lying – you think he's mistaken."

"It wouldn't be the first time," Young noted and began to list the facts, counting them off on his fingers as he went.

"It was dark. The kid was leading his first combat patrol. He's new in theater, new to action, and new to the area. His squad encounters a couple of Russian soldiers and eliminates them. It's only natural he would be hyped up on adrenaline, right?"

"I guess," the Army Intelligence Captain conceded.

"And then we have logic. Look at the situation. The Russians are methodical and predictable. They attack *en masse*. Ponting's report – if it were accurate – would mean that the enemy has been stealthily moving an advance element of troops and armor across the border and massing them without ever being detected by our satellites."

"Is it possible?"

"Well… yes," Young shrugged his shoulders and conceded. "We're covering a hell of a lot of battlefield with limited assets… But it wouldn't fit with the typical Russian *Modus operandi*."

"But it is possible…"

"Anything is possible. It's war," Young blustered. "But even the Lieutenant's Company commander, Captain Gatfield, doesn't believe the report."

"You interviewed him?"

"Briefly, by phone. Apparently, our Lieutenant Ponting caused a scene at a high-level Allied liaison meeting about information he received from a couple of village locals. The Captain described Ponting as 'rude and excitable'."

"So, what action do you recommend we take?"

Major Young considered the question for a long moment, the Battalion S2's face working as he wrestled with the delicate issue. Finally, he gave a gusty sigh, his decision made. "Bury the Lieutenant's report."

"And his request for supplies and equipment?"

"I'll make sure we send him everything he requisitioned. Maybe it will convince him we've taken his intelligence seriously. Let the dust settle. We're in a war, after all. In a week's time there will be a new crisis brewing and the Lieutenant's little corner of the Kaliningrad-Lithuania Line won't matter anymore."

*

The western wall of the room had been crumbled by an artillery shell, the tiled roof partially collapsed. There were blood stains and scorch marks on the timber floor. In the center of the room stood a simple wooden table, pitted and notched and worn. A small fuel lamp, it's light flickering, illuminated a map of the Suwalki Gap region of northern Poland.

The three-star Colonel general of tanks who had been given the burden of commanding the Russian assault through the Kaliningrad-Lithuania Line walked solemnly from the table to a shattered window and stared out at the muddy fields beyond the farmhouse. When at last he spoke, his voice sounded hollow with despair.

"Have the American's begun reinforcing their positions?"

"No, sir."

"Do we have fresh satellite imagery of the region?" The Colonel general turned from the window to look at the table where two pale-faced Russian officers stood.

"The latest batch from Intelligence are six hours old, sir. They show no Allied movement anywhere along their lines."

"Six hours?" the Colonel general protested, his voice harsh. "When will there be another overhead pass?"

Beyond the broken glass of the window the farm fields were churned and pitted with artillery craters. The farm was located just two miles on the Lithuanian side of the border. The building had been bomb-damaged and abandoned during the early days of the Baltic invasion. Now it was headquarters for the Russian attack force that was massing behind a dense wall of forest to the northwest.

"Not for another eight hours," one of the officers delivered the news.

The Colonel general sighed, wrestling with a problem.

Two days earlier an American patrol had scouted a forest to the northeast of the village of Szelment where the Russians had been assembling an advance assault force. Two Russian sentries had been killed before the Americans were engaged in a firefight and fled. One US soldier had been killed in the action, but the rest had escaped to a small outpost northeast of Becejty.

The question upon which the fate of the impending Russia attack rested was simple: *had the Americans scouting the forest stumbled upon the ranks of armored personnel carriers and tanks concealed in the forest?*

"We can be assured the American scouts were chased out of the woods long before they could discover our force," one of the officers at the table predicted confidently. "Otherwise, the entire Allied line would be on high alert by now."

"I agree, sir," the second officer said. "At the very least the road from Warsaw would be choked with American armor moving north. We've seen nothing on satellite to suggest that is the case."

"So, you're confident the Americans have not uncovered our plans?" the Colonel general was not convinced. "The Americans are a cunning, clever adversary. We could be charging into a trap."

"If we allow ourselves to be cowered, cautious and timid, we will invite disaster," the first officer ventured in oblique reproof.

It was rare for a junior officer to so directly challenge the authority of a Colonel general, yet the war was going badly for the Russians and discipline and morale within the ranks had been shaken. The ignominious Russian retreat from Warsaw had frayed tempers and eroded order.

The Colonel general smiled thinly, baring his teeth at the man who had challenged him. "I wonder, Major Kaminchov, if you would be so blithe with your comments if it was your head on the chopping block – if it was you who must face the President should our push through the Allied lines be rebuffed?"

"I apologize," the junior officer bobbed his head dutifully. "I meant no offense, Colonel general, I was merely quoting from doctrine –"

"Ah, yes," the Colonel general's eyes turned wolfish and his voice became sour with contempt. "I forget that you are a textbook soldier, Major. You have not yet fought in battle, correct?"

"That is true, sir, but –"

"We shall remedy this. I know you must be keen to apply all you have learned from your books to real fighting at the front. So, I will issue you fresh orders immediately to ensure you are posted to our frontline units that form the spearhead of our drive through the enemy's defenses."

The Major's face turned ashen. The Colonel general's face hardened in savage retribution. "You are dismissed. I suggest you return immediately to your quarters to pack your belongings, Major. I will arrange a vehicle to transport you to your new posting." The Major retreated, shaken, from the room. The Colonel general swung his focus to the remaining officer by the table like he was taking aim. The man swallowed and stiffened. "Has there been any word from Yesenin?"

"The *zampolit* Captain (political commissar) is already en route back from Western Operational Strategic Command headquarters, sir. He is due to arrive at any moment."

"Good," the Colonel general took one long last look at the map spread across the tabletop and frowned. He questioned if he should bring forward the attack, then almost immediately dismissed the notion. The assault was scheduled for dawn in two days' time. The troops and tanks could not be mobilized any earlier.

When the attack launched, he wondered whether he would be springing a trap… or stumbling into one.

*

The Black Hawk touched down smoothly and Guy Ponting leaped from the cargo bay into the chopper's dust-swirling downdraught. His landing on the hard sunbaked earth shot a jolt of pain up his injured arm. He winced, then straightened. Sergeant Harley stood at the edge of the LZ to greet the Lieutenant.

"Glad you're not dead, sir."

"So am I. You'll need more men to help unload the helicopter."

He led the Sergeant back to the Black Hawk and gestured at the open cargo bay like he had arrived bearing gifts.

"Jesus, Mary, mother of God!" Sergeant Harley's face lit up in surprise and satisfaction. The belly of the Black Hawk was stacked with a dozen heavy crates. "What the hell…?" the big man had to shout above the beating *'thwack, thwack, thwack'* of the rotors to be heard.

"Another 50cal heavy machine gun, all the ammunition we need and more Claymores," Lieutenant Ponting said. "There is another Black Hawk due in about an hour. It's carrying more ammunition, batteries for our night vision gear, C-wire for the perimeter, and the spare parts we requested for the Humvee."

Sergeant Harley turned, put his fingers to his lips and whistled. Several men inside the barricade came running through the gap in the wire to unload the cargo.

Harley and Ponting left the heavy lifting to the troops. Ponting's injured arm still hung in a sling, clutched to his side like a broken wing. Sergeant Harley gestured at the Lieutenant's shoulder. "Should you be back here so soon?"

"I gotta be somewhere," Ponting shrugged off the question. "And the wound is as good as healed."

They walked together through the compound, inspecting the perimeter. Several of the men on sentry duty greeted Ponting with grins and good-natured nods of acknowledgement. When they reached the northern corner of the outpost, Sergeant Harley stopped and cast his eyes towards the border, suddenly grave and serious.

The villages of Postawelek and Szelment lay beneath the shadow of a drifting cloud bank.

He gestured with a jerk of his head. "There's trouble brewing," Harley opined. "The Russians are too quiet and it makes me nervous. An attack is coming, Lieutenant; I can feel it. Normally we can hear enemy artillery, pounding Allied positions to the north, or we'll see Russian fighters patrolling the border. But in the days since you were evacuated, the entire Kaliningrad-Lithuania Line has gone silent. It's eerie."

"Well, you have nothing to worry about, Sergeant," Lieutenant Ponting reassured the troubled veteran. "I spoke to Battalion and Army Intelligence in Warsaw. They came to my hospital bed. The Army now knows about the enemy armor concealed in the forest and they are aware the Russians have some small force hiding in Szelment. If the enemy had plans to launch an assault, they've probably abandoned them now that they realize they have lost any element of surprise. And if they do come? Then we'll be ready for them. By now I imagine there are columns of Abrams MBTs already streaming north from Warsaw to reinforce us. The Russians had their chance, and they missed it. The entire Allied Army from here to Kaliningrad will be resupplied, armed and on full alert." He turned and peered over his shoulder as though he expected to see a rising trail of dust on the road from Warsaw, announcing the advance of Allied armor, even as he spoke. He saw nothing.

"Well, I hope the word filters down to Company HQ in a hurry, Lieutenant," Sergeant Harley said ominously. "Because Captain Gatfield still has not ordered the fortification of Becejty. He hasn't even blocked off the roads leading to the village."

"He hasn't?" Ponting felt the first stirring of uncertainty.

"No, sir."

Ponting frowned. It was possible orders about a potential Russian attack were still trickling down from NATO command. It was possible too, that Army Intelligence had detected enemy troop movements further to the north or south of their positions and deemed the valley that Fort Suicide overlooked as a low-risk region.

Ponting picked up a pair of binoculars. He focused the lenses and stared back at Becejty, nestled near the banks of the lake. He could see civilians on the streets and several Army trucks, but no signs of activity, or of local citizens being evacuated. He raised the binoculars a little and refocused them on the horizon. The roads and fields southwest towards Warsaw were empty. The sky too was devoid of military aircraft. Ponting had expected the air would be filled with transports and helicopters bringing troops forward beneath the umbrella of fighter cover…

Ponting put down the glasses and felt a sick slide of foreboding.

Had Major Young from Army Intelligence ignored his report?

The prospect made him physically ill. He snatched up the binoculars again and studied the skyline towards Warsaw more intently. The galling truth of the situation struck him at last.

It was a nightmare.

The bleak reality was, that with forty men and no immediate support, they were marooned on the Poland-Lithuanian border staring down the prospect of an imminent multi-division-strength enemy attack.

Lieutenant Ponting spun on his heel and raised his voice to a shout. "Skinner? Get Battalion HQ on the line. Immediately!"

*

A commotion at the outpost's southwestern perimeter roused Lieutenant Ponting from a fitful sleep. He rolled off the narrow cot and came slowly to his feet, the pain in his shoulder throbbing. He discarded the sling, and was surprised that he had good mobility in his arm despite the nagging pain. He flexed his shoulder like a swimmer warming up on the starting blocks and stepped out into the compound.

It was late afternoon. The sun hung low in a sky turning orange and purple and golden with the approach of sunset.

Ponting strode towards the wire where a soldier was on sentry duty, his weapon raised and aimed as a precaution.

"Problem, Private?"

"Three civilians approaching from Becejty, Lieutenant," the soldier jerked his head. Ponting looked down the slope, following the dirt road towards the village. An elderly man and two young girls were at the bottom of the rise, the girls walking slowly to match the pace of the elderly man.

"Go and escort them in."

The soldier slung his weapon and went down the trail while Ponting watched on. There was a brief exchange between the soldier and the civilians and then they leaned into the slope, scuffing up little clouds of dust with their feet as they made the ascent. The soldier held the old man's arm, steadying him as the incline taxed his stamina.

At the breach in the wire, Ponting saw the two girls were in fact teenagers. One had long blonde hair, a slim athletic figure and a serious expression. The other girl appeared a little younger. She had dark hair and a plain unremarkable face. Sergeant Wagner came striding across the compound and leaned close to the Lieutenant.

"Sir, these are the two girls my patrol encountered in the woods – they're the ones who relayed the information about the Russians in Szelment." He nodded to the two Polish teenagers and beckoned the trooper who spoke German. "They don't speak English. Harris can interpret for you."

The old man was dressed in a faded, dusty black suit that was worn at the elbows and frayed around the collar. Atop his head was a wide-brimmed hat. He was very old, his face splotched with livid marks, his skin creased and worn as an old pair of boots. He took a fresh linen handkerchief from his top pocket and mopped his brow.

"I speak English," he said. His voice was rusty with age, wavering and brittle. He held out his hand and bowed with old-world courtesy. "I am Tadeusz Pwlikowska," he introduced himself.

Ponting shook hands. The old Polish man's flesh was thin and dry as parchment. "And these are my granddaughters, Wislawa and Urszula."

Ponting nodded politely. The girls stood close to the old man as though intimidated by the presence of the soldiers.

"I am Lieutenant Guy Ponting, commander of Combat Outpost Bravo Zero-Six. Would you like to sit for a moment?" he asked the old man.

Tadeusz Pwlikowska shook his head. He took off his hat and fanned his face. His head was bald. "I have information for your Generals," the Polish man said. "You must share with them everything I have seen, yes?"

"Of course," Ponting nodded again.

The old man looked convinced. His eyes were rheumy and pale beneath bushy grey brows. He gazed down at his dirt covered shoes for a moment as if wondering where to start. "I live in Szelment," he began. "I have lived there all my life, and I tell you the village is occupied by Russian soldiers."

"How do you know this?" Ponting showed no great surprise.

"They are on the street," the old man said. "But they are wearing the clothes of civilians. Yet it is obvious they are not locals."

"Could they be tourists?"

"No," the old man scoffed. "There are no tourists visiting northern Poland in the midst of a war. And there are too many of them; too many young men with military haircuts speaking faulty Polish."

"How many?"

Tadeusz Pwlikowska shrugged. "Perhaps as many as a hundred."

"What do you think they are doing in your village?" Ponting asked.

The old man gave a sudden knowing smile and then his expression turned foxy. "They are keeping people from visiting the nearby forest," he said. "I know this because there are men on the road leading from the village. They carry no weapons but they are intimidating the locals. Normally the forest is popular in summer. There are family outings to the woods and picnics. Children play games of *'Chowanego'* amongst the trees. But now the young men in the village prohibit anyone from travelling in that direction."

"You believe there is something hidden in the forest?"

The old man shrugged, then lowered his voice to a conspiratorial whisper so that his granddaughters would not overhear. "Two days ago, a local man and a young woman were found dead in their home. No one knows how they died, but there is a rumor that they went to the forest at night the way that young lovers have always done. The next morning their bodies were discovered."

"What about Postawelek?" Sergeant Davin Wagner pointed to the village that lay two kilometers away, positioned between the outpost and Szelment. "Have you heard anything about Russian troops there?"

The old man shook his head. "I have a friend who lives there," he said. "We play chess in the village square on Sundays. He has said nothing."

Ponting drew a deep breath and considered the old man's information. The sun was setting quickly, the day turning to twilight. He had learned nothing new from the old man, yet his story had corroborated his own information.

"How long are you staying with your granddaughters in Becejty?"

"Until tomorrow."

Ponting looked pained. "There is an American Company headquarters in the village, commanded by a man named Captain Gatfield. Would you repeat to him what you have just told me if I can arrange for you to speak to him?"

Tadeusz Pwlikowska shrugged. "Of course."

Ponting smiled his thanks and then arranged for a soldier to drive the old man and the girls back to the village. "Take them to Company HQ," he instructed. "I'll have RTO Skinner radio ahead to see if the Captain will take the meeting."

Chapter 5:

At sunrise the following morning the Platoon paraded and were broken up into several work details. Sergeant Wagner handed six men trenching tools and told them to begin filling sandbags. Sergeant Harley led ten men down the northern slope of the knoll and began sewing the ground beyond the outpost with Claymore mines connected through a concealed network of firing wire. The troops labored through the morning, their shirts off, their bodies glistening with sweat as the sun moved across the sky and morning gave way to the stifling heat of a summer afternoon.

Within the compound, Guy Ponting supervised a team of soldiers who repaired the concertina wire around the perimeter and then added a second roll to increase the height of the barrier. Sheets of thin armor plate were hoisted to the deck of the watchtower and laid against the wall facing north to protect the machine gun crew from Russian small arms fire.

Once the soldiers were immersed in their tasks, Ponting detached himself from the work and set about preparing a 'standard range card' for each key position around the base's perimeter so that if the Russians attacked in darkness or from behind a wall of smoke, the soldiers would know instantly how to orient the Platoon's heavy weapons towards the most likely approaches. As he sketched the terrain in front of each position, he made sure to include the prominent features and mark areas of dead ground. Working with a compass and map, he calculated the azimuth in degrees from each gun position to the prominent terrain features, then reckoned ranges. It was painstaking, methodical work that required concentration. When the Lieutenant looked up at last, the men carrying trenching tools were beginning to move the filled sandbags into position.

The sandbags were stacked in front of re-dug trenches and the gaps in the wire at each corner of the compound closed. Ammunition was distributed to each forward-facing trench and two firing positions for the Javelin anti-tank teams were built with the protection of a waist-high barricade of logs, mud and sandbags.

Ponting supervised the laying of the first sandbags. Once the work was proceeding he retreated to the shade of his bunker to complete a 'Platoon Sketch Card'. The sector sketch marked where the Platoon's weapons would be oriented and detailed the terrain across the shallow valley. He plotted in the position of the Claymores, then set the card aside and by the fading light of late afternoon at last turned his attention to the battlefield sketch, mapping and coding each Target Reference Point (TRP) between the outpost and the village of Postawelek. He labored over the task with painstaking attention to detail, knowing that the time spent could save men's lives if the Russians attacked.

"Skinner!" he studied the finished battlefield sketch a final time while he waited for the RTO to appear.

When Skinner arrived, he was filthy with dirt and sweat. Ponting handed the radio operator the battlefield sketch. "I want this sent up to Company and Battalion immediately," he said, "With a request that the Battalion Fires Officer sends copies to every designated support artillery unit in our sector. Understand?"

Skinner nodded, took the sketch, and disappeared in a cloud of stale body odor.

The work around the base continued until sunset, and resumed after nightfall. The sandbags that revetted the walls of the Lieutenant's bunker were carried to the perimeter wall and used instead to reinforce the trenches. Then fire steps were built at the bottom of each ditch. The trenches facing north towards the villages in the distance were joined until they became one long zig-zagging ditch that stretched from the northwest corner of the outpost to the southeast corner. Ponting stood on the lip of the earthwork and was reminded of the WW1 trenches that had criss-crossed Belgium and northern France at the height of the Great War. The front wall of the ditch was reinforced with more sandbags and a series of upright posts that would protect the excavation from collapse against Russian artillery.

Ammunition and grenades were stored at several points along the trench line along with a box of flares.

At sunset, Lieutenant Ponting ordered the network of Claymore mines close to the perimeter dug up and moved further down the slope. "If they get this close to the perimeter, we will already be dead and the compound overrun," he reasoned. "And there's no chance of the Russians surprising us with armor… so move the mines down into the foot of the valley where they can make a difference."

The soldiers finished the work by torchlight and trudged back to the camp, tired and exhausted. They threw themselves down on the ground and drank greedily from their canteens. Sergeant Harley steered Ponting away from the men until they were standing alone, facing out across the darkening valley. In the night sky the first stars emerged and a slice of moon rose from behind the horizon.

"Have you ever lived through an earthquake, Lieutenant?"

Ponting shook his head, bemused.

"I have," Sergeant Harley said. His voice was hushed and sounded tinged with superstition as he spoke. "I lived in Los Angeles for a time before I joined the Army and one night I was with a girl in a park on the outskirts of the city. We were looking up at the night sky and the trees were filled with nature, y'know? Birds and crickets and shit. But suddenly it went real quiet. I mean *real* quiet. The birds and the critters stopped chirping. It was eerie. It was like the world was suddenly holding its breath, waiting for something ominous to happen. Fifteen seconds later an earthquake shook the city." The Sergeant lapsed into sudden silence and stood brooding into the darkening night.

For several seconds Guy Ponting said nothing. Finally, he shrugged his shoulders. "So? What's your point, Sergeant?"

"Listen," Harley whispered. "Tell me what you hear."

Ponting cocked his ear dutifully and concentrated. He could hear nothing other than the muttered desultory conversation of the soldiers. Beyond the perimeter of Fort Suicide, the night was deathly quiet.

*

Ponting called a meeting of his Sergeants and the men assembled in the bunker. He had a map of the local terrain overhanging the edges of his cot and he studied it thoughtfully.

"We're on our own until the Russians start pounding the front with artillery and the first tanks appear on the horizon. That much we know because Army Intelligence, Battalion command, and Captain Gatfield all refuse to believe the intelligence reports. So…" he looked up from the map and searched the faces of the men around him. "If you were the Russians looking to punch a hole in the Kaliningrad-Lithuania Line through the valley to our north, how would you go about the assault?"

"They could overwhelm us with a night attack," one of the Sergeants voiced his personal fear.

Ponting considered the possibility. The majority of Russian units, he decided, would most likely be made up of fresh troops, perhaps still unblooded in combat. The enemy were simply stretched too thin on too many fronts to have the luxury of redeploying several divisions of veteran soldiers from other sectors for the assault. That made Ponting doubt the Russian Generals in command would risk a night attack even though he conceded such a tactic could bring swift victory. The downside was that night operations were invariably messy, confused conflicts – not the kind of battle suited to raw recruits, or ranks recently transported to the front without extensive combat experience.

"I don't think so," Ponting explained his reasoning. "However, the troops in Szelment might be tasked to the operation. They would know the area, and they might even be Spetsnaz. But a company of elite special forces operatives isn't going to be enough to punch through Allied lines, not without a lot of armor and artillery in support."

"It will be a dawn attack," Sergeant Harley predicted. "The Russians always attack at dawn because it gives them an entire day to exploit their advantage."

"Dawn tomorrow?"

Harley shrugged. "It's possible," he remembered the eerie stillness of the night that he believed to be a harbinger of impending catastrophe.

Ponting considered the possibility and became assailed by bleak and pessimistic doubts. His Platoon of men, isolated from support, faced an enemy that might be a hundred times their own number. The Russians would have tanks, APCs and artillery, while Ponting had just two dozen Javelin anti-tank missiles and a couple of launchers, supplemented by four AT-4 single-shot weapons.

"Perhaps Army Intelligence will read the signs and Command will act in time," Davin Wagner said. "The longer the Russians delay their attack, the more chance there is that their security will be compromised and their plan discovered."

"Good point," Ponting tried to muster some enthusiasm, but could not.

When the men were dismissed, Ponting walked to the northwestern corner of the compound. He stood there, alone, staring down into the shallow valley and worried what the next day would bring.

The wind rose, chill across the elevated ground, and then veered around to the east until he detected the faint odor of smoke on the night air. He thought he heard, carried on the gusting breeze, the far away rumble of an engine. He closed his eyes, trying to isolate the noise yet it drifted away and never came again.

He retreated to his bunker and threw himself down on the cot. It was after midnight and he was physically and mentally exhausted yet he lay awake, anxious and overwrought, assailed by problems too momentous for solutions.

*

A sudden flurry of automatic weapons fire ripped through the night and jarred Lieutenant Ponting and every other man to instant alert.

Ponting glanced at his watch as he tumbled from the cot; it was 0200 hours. He blundered about in the dark for a moment, pulling on his boots, and then scampered up the bunker's steps and into the cold dark night.

More chattering gunfire sounded, this time from further along the northern trench.

"Hold your fire!" Ponting bellowed the order and heard his command echoed by a Sergeant from somewhere in the night. He ran to the trench and peered into the deep hole. A Private on sentry duty lifted his pale face. His expression was embarrassed and apologetic.

"Sorry, Lieutenant. I thought I saw something move down in the valley floor, about two hundred yards due north."

Ponting peered into the gloom. He neither heard nor saw anything. He sent Sergeant Harley around the perimeter with a warning that no man was to open fire without direct orders. The man on sentry duty reloaded his weapon.

"If the Russians launch an attack, we'll all hear it," Ponting said.

Slowly, the men off-duty returned to their bunkers and the commotion around the outpost settled. Ponting lingered. He climbed the ladder to the watchtower and spoke briefly to the two men hunched over the heavy machine gun. The night air was chilled by a fretful breeze that made the sounds of the night difficult to discern. He thought he heard the *'clink!'* of metal against metal, from somewhere out in the dark night, but was not sure. Whatever the sound was, it was too small, and too far away, to be significant. He leaned close to the man hunched over the machine gun. "Seen anything?"

"Nothing," the gunner grunted. At his feet were two spare cartridge boxes and a handful of M127A1 handheld parachute illumination devices. Ponting peered beyond the wall of sandbags and through the draped curtain of camouflage netting. The sky was filled with stars but the moon was obscured by low scudding cloud. He considered ordering a flare to be fired and then reluctantly decided against the notion. It was important he project an aura of confidence. Filling the night sky with flares would appear the action of a man prone to panic. So instead, he went quickly back down the ladder and moved around the perimeter, pausing to talk with the men pulling sentry duty until the tension seemed to have passed and quiet calm had returned.

To his surprise he encountered Sergeant Harley standing close to the camouflage covered Humvee. The Sergeant stood with a cigarette dangling from the corner of his mouth, peering north.

"Can't sleep?" Ponting made small talk.

The Sergeant shook his head and plucked the cigarette from between his lips. "Can't wait," he muttered. "I just want the bastards to attack so we can get it over with. It's not the fighting that bothers me – it's the damned waiting."

Ponting grunted. "An English fiction writer and poet by the name of Sarah Doudney summed it up best. She said, *'The waiting time, my brothers, is the hardest time of all.'*"

"Amen to that," Sergeant Harley said, and crushed the butt of his cigarette beneath the heel of his boot.

*

"Once we have captured the village of Becejty, NATO theater Command will have a difficult decision to make," the Russian Colonel general remarked to Captain Yesenin. The Colonel tried to hide his contempt for the *zampolit* Captain behind a scowling expression, but conceded that it was important the political officer understood the tactical situation and fully appreciated his own cunning brilliance.

The *zampolit* was an oily, short-statured man with reptilian eyes and a docile sickly expression that concealed a ruthless political ambition. He had arrived back from Western Operational Strategic Command just thirty minutes earlier and was keen to be briefed on the plans for the coming campaign. The Colonel general had no doubt that every word uttered in this meeting would be relayed back to Moscow. Yesenin served Russia's political masters, not the Army.

"Are you certain of victory?" Yesenin's eyes swept over the maps strewn across the farmhouse table. It was late at night but beyond the walls of the building the cobblestoned courtyard was a hive of activity as headquarters staff finalized the battle orders for the assault that would commence in just a few short hours' time.

"Yes," the Colonel general nodded.

Yesenin smiled. A crushing victory would force NATO back onto the defensive in northern Europe and leave Poland vulnerable for re-invasion. Once Warsaw had been re-taken, the ground offensive in Ukraine could be stalled long enough for Russia to bring all its considerable military power to bear against the stubborn Germans. And after Berlin fell..? By then Captain Yesenin would be a *zampolit* Major with a small office in a corner of the Kremlin and access to the corridors of his nation's political power. It would be a spectacular ascent to the upper echelons of influence for a man who had been born and raised in the gutters of Nizhny Novgorod.

"Is there more you would want to know?" the Colonel general prompted the *zampolit* who had drifted into a daydream.

"Yes," Captain Yesenin nodded. "You said the enemy's commanders would be faced with a decision once we break through. I would like to know what choices NATO will have once Becejty has fallen."

The Colonel general leaned over the map and made a broad sweeping gesture with his hand. "Once our armor has severed the Allied line, the NATO defenses will be split in half. Their Generals must then decide whether to abandon the northern end of the line or to withdraw and surrender their position along the border. If they abandon the line, our forces will encircle their positions and we will hunt the remnants of their Army down and crush them."

"And if they withdraw, back towards Warsaw?"

"That would be an even greater mistake," the Colonel general bared his teeth like a shark about to feed. "For then we would be able to fight a fluid, mobile campaign against an enemy without set defensive positions to hide behind. Once the NATO troops are dislodged from their trenches and hills, they will be given no rest. Our motorized rifle brigades will pursue them, our mobile artillery will give them no respite, and our tanks will be able to drive unobstructed all the way to Warsaw. NATO's doctrine has always been built around defending. But in order to defend a position you need time and structure, Yesenin. If we can keep them off balance, and if we can rob them of opportunities to stabilize the breach, they will become fodder for our guns."

The *zampolit* Captain nodded. The Colonel general of tanks spoke with confidence and assurance. Yesenin had never served in the military, yet even he could understand the strategic situation. He flashed the Colonel a thin smile of admiration, but then added a note of caution.

"The NATO troops pushed us back from the German border…" he pointed out.

"No!" the Colonel general said hotly. "We broke ourselves on their guns, Yesenin. We over-extended ourselves without an adequate supply line and without sufficient troops for the task. Once we exhausted ourselves attacking the NATO defensive positions, they merely counter-attacked. We beat ourselves. That will not happen here."

The *zampolit* nodded in concession. He glowered over the map and focused his attention on Becejty, situated close to the border. It lay at the southern end of a shallow valley of farmland on the tip of a stretch of lake, just a scant three kilometers from the highway to Suwalki. He tapped the map with the tip of his finger. "Why have you chosen this particular place to break through the Allied lines?" he leaned closer. "Why Becejty?"

"Because Intelligence tells us the area is only lightly defended by a single company of American troops – some are deployed in the village itself, and some are defending an outpost a kilometer further north."

"Are you sure you can make the breakthrough there?"

The Colonel smiled bleakly. "We already have a Battalion of tanks concealed in woods across the Polish border, just north of the village, as well as a Battalion of APCs. Once the attack begins at dawn tomorrow a further full Division of armor and infantry will stream into that valley, Yesenin; an entire Division against a Company of American infantry who are unsupported by armor. How long do you think they will hold us up? Ten minutes? Less than that, I think," the Colonel general dismissed the question with contempt. "We attack at dawn and by breakfast the village will be overrun and our tanks will be on the highway to Suwalki."

Captain Yesenin was not a military man, yet even he had to concede that the numbers in favor of the assault force were overwhelming. He beamed his admiration, aware that his future too rested on the Colonel general's shoulders. As *zampolit*, his own career path was inextricably tied to the success of the operation. Technically he was responsible for the patriotic spirit amongst the soldiers, their morale, and their political education. In reality he was answerable to Moscow for the performance of the attack force's military leadership. The Colonel general's decisions reflected on him and his assessments.

"Your victory will be cause for great celebration in the streets of Moscow, Colonel general," the Captain fawned. "I'm sure there will be more medals to reward your valor, and perhaps even another star on your lapel."

The Colonel general of tanks looked distinctly unimpressed. "I don't care about medals, Yesenin. It's the Polish women that interest me. These Lithuanians…" he screwed up his face with revulsion, "… are too fat and too damn greasy for my tastes. Have you seen their faces? They're a surly, distinctly ugly people. I can't tell the females from the men, for God's sakes. No! I want some young tender Polish flesh," he rubbed his hands together and smiled a lecherous grin of carnal anticipation. "Some beautiful Warsaw girls with firm round breasts to keep my bed warm and my cock hard."

The *zampolit* blanched and hid his distaste. He managed a grunt and a short snickering laugh. The Colonel arched his eyebrows in a challenge.

"You don't care for female company, Yesenin?"

"I don't obsess over sex, Colonel general," the *zampolit* said with tight restraint.

"Well, my men do, Yesenin. That's all they care about. And you're the political officer, yes? Well, if you want to ensure a victory tomorrow, you should spread the rumor that a thousand pretty Polish girls are visiting that shit-hole little village we're attacking for a bikini beauty contest. Morale will be lifted sky-high, and in the morning the men will burst through brick walls for a chance to be first behind the American lines."

*

The entire Platoon were roused from their bunks at 0400 hours in the morning and ordered to man the perimeter. It was still pitch black, the dawn more than an hour away. Men stood to their posts, muttering quietly to each other while coffee was brewed and MREs heated. The air smelled of damp grass and drifting smoke. Someone coughed and the noise of it was harsh and jarringly loud in the stifled quiet.

Lieutenant Ponting stood at the foot of the watchtower and lifted binoculars to his eyes. There was a smear of smoke against the starlit horizon and a faint glow of light along the rim of the eastern skyline. Ponting focused the glasses on the distant village of Szelment and saw the lights of the settlement burning brightly. He frowned and felt a sick slide of foreboding. He swung the binoculars again until the village of Postawelek slid into view. The township remained dark as a graveyard. In the fields close to the outpost Ponting could see the long grass had been brushed flat by overnight wind.

A Private handed Ponting a tin mug of coffee, then joined the rest of the men in the north-facing trench. The Lieutenant sipped at the steaming liquid and began a slow circuit around the perimeter. He found Sergeant Davin Wagner in a section of deep trench at the southeastern corner of the compound.

A sudden gust of cold damp air swept over the exposed ground and then it began to rain. The men in the trench hunched down, cold and miserable while the bottom of the narrow, sandbagged pit began to turn muddy. Sergeant Wagner pretended the surroundings were a paradise compared to the conditions he had endured during the first siege of Warsaw. Two of the other men who had fought in the Polish capital echoed the Sergeant's claims while the soldiers with less combat experience stopped grumbling.

The men in the trench made space for Ponting, and he slid down into the muddy pit. The trench was head-high and about four feet wide; narrow enough to protect the men from anything other than a direct artillery strike, and wide enough for a man to stand on the fire step and shoot while another stood behind him, from where he could either move along the line to a vulnerable point, or reload.

A small fire had been built at the bottom of the pit, and although it afforded no warmth, it gave the men small light to see each other and orientate themselves in the dark.

"Do you think this is the day, Lieutenant?" one of the younger soldiers in the group could not conceal his anxiety.

"We'll know soon enough," Ponting said grimly. He checked the dial of his watch. "Dawn in a few minutes."

"Do you think we'll get support, sir? I mean, once the Russian artillery starts shelling the line, Battalion will know the enemy are mounting an attack. They'll have to come to our aid then, right?" a Corporal with an intelligent, earnest expression reasoned.

"Of course," Ponting nodded. "All we have to do is hold our position. Once Battalion realizes our intelligence reports were right all along, they'll mobilize everything they have immediately to support the sectors under assault." In truth

Ponting was not so sure Battalion HQ would act with the alacrity he hoped, but it was his job to give these men confidence they were not entirely isolated. Some of the men from further along the trench edged closer to listen. "We just have to hold off the initial Russian thrust – if it comes," he assured them in a loud voice. "Maybe the enemy have abandoned their offensive, or re-deployed further north."

"I was deployed on the eastern outskirts of Warsaw when the Russians first attacked back in May," Sergeant Davin Wagner looked up into the rain filled night. The water was puddling in the hollows around the compound and running in rivulets down the walls of the trench. "My Company was defending a row of houses at a place called Zabki, east of the Vistula River," his voice turned dark and introspective as if he were seeing the location in his mind as he spoke. "The day before the Russians had reached as far west as Zielonka, a town about thirteen clicks north east of Warsaw. We were damned sure they were going to roll right over us come sunrise, so the Captain got on the radio to Battalion and told them we were facing armor and APCs, and that we needed reinforcements."

"What happened?" one of the men on the fringe of the group asked. Everyone had become hushed, listening avidly to the Sergeant's story.

Davin Wagner looked suddenly haunted. His eyes became huge and dark. "The Russians came alright. As dawn approached, we could hear their tanks, engines roaring as they trundled down the road towards our positions behind a barrage of artillery. We had been promised that a Company of Abrams were on their way to support us, but they never arrived."

"What happened?" another man prompted when the Sergeant's voice trailed into momentary silence.

"We broke," Wagner said with a flush of red-faced humiliation. "The Russians outnumbered us ten-to-one, and all we had to fight back with was our M4s and a couple of Javelins. Most of the unit were slaughtered where they stood.

A handful of us survived. When we finally made it back to Battalion HQ, the Captain walked up to the Lieutenant Colonel in command and punched him flush in the face. The Colonel was lucky the Captain got to him first. I would have killed the bastard…"

Suddenly the far-off distance became filled with noise. It overshadowed the sound of the drumming rain until it seemed to swell across the eastern horizon. The men held their breath and strained their ears.

"Oh, Christ…" one soldier muttered. He pointed through a gap in the wall of sandbags. The rim of the world seemed to be alight and flickering with a furious red glow. A deep rumble shook the frigid air.

A moment later the first Russian artillery shells began landing in the farm fields north of Fort Suicide.

Chapter 6:

The first Russian artillery rounds arced above the clouds, sounding like rolling thunder across the dawn sky. Ponting snatched for a pair of binoculars and saw the horizon streaked with thin grey tendrils of smoke. He followed the trajectory of one shell and watched it explode somewhere amidst a tangle of narrow alleys on the western outskirts of Postawelek. A few seconds later the entire village seemed to erupt in flames. Ponting gazed, transfixed. The village's church tower collapsed in a cloud of dust and debris and then a building near the main intersection exploded, its roof collapsing, the walls blowing outwards.

"Christ!" Ponting breathed, awe-struck by the devastation being wrought. For a long moment he could see nothing but swirling smoke and dust. Then the haze thinned and he noticed grey ghost-like figures, moving amidst the rubble and devastation. They were visible for just a moment, then were snatched away as more rounds plunged down from the sky.

The ground trembled and the air seemed to quiver with the shrieking howls of imminent death. The pounding Russian batteries buried the village beneath a pile of shattered rubble.

When the guns abruptly fell silent, the soldiers defending Fort Suicide carefully raised their heads and gaped in awe-struck horror at the scene of devastation. Every man had seen combat before, but none had witnessed the thundering power of massed Russian artillery. Of Postawelek, nothing remained. The entire settlement had been obliterated from the face of the earth. The fields surrounding the village were churned to upheaved and cratered mounds of earth, and the meandering road that once led to the village had simply ceased to exist.

The choking cloud of smoke drifted on the breeze, reducing visibility and blanketing the shallow valley beneath the COP in a dirty fog-like haze.

"Prepare for action!" Guy Ponting stood on the fire step and cupped his hands to his mouth to shout. His ears were ringing from the fury of the Russian barrage so that his voice sounded strangely muted. He peered hard into the drifting skeins of haze. He could see movement around the village of Szelment, but it was too vague and indistinct behind the veil of smoke for him to define. He swung the glasses onto the elongated stretch of forest where the patrol had first spotted the concealed Russian tanks and APCs. Nothing moved.

"Get your damned head down!" Platoon Sergeant Harley came hustling along the trench. He seized Ponting by the scruff of his tunic and pulled him to the bottom of the muddy pit. "The Russians are just changing their aim," he hissed.

As if the man had some direct psychic link to the Gods of War, the enemy chose that very moment to resume their artillery barrage. Now the massed guns began concentrating their fire on the village of Becejty.

One of the soldiers crouched low in the trench and began to mouth the words to a prayer. Another man crossed himself and plucked a photo of his wife from his pocket. The sky overhead filled with the deafening whine of artillery shells as they arced through the air; a thunderous cacophony of fire and fury that sounded like the end of the world.

"Everybody down!" Sergeant Harley had to shout himself hoarse to be heard over the maelstrom.

Lieutenant Ponting endured the barrage, shivering and quietly terrified, hunched deep in the shelter of the trench. It seemed impossible to him that anything could survive the relentless ground-rumbling fury of the explosions. His senses were overwhelmed until he felt physically dazed. No one in the trenches spoke. The thunder of the screaming shells drowned out all other sounds.

When the artillery barrage finally stopped, the men rose from the depths of their trenches like survivors of some cataclysmic holocaust. Their faces were smeared with sweat and spattered mud, their eyes red-rimmed by smoke. They stared south and through the dust saw bright red pinpricks of flickering flames. The lake beside the village of Becejty was black with ash, the roads leading into and out of the settlement were cratered, and the land churned brown. The village itself was little more than a black charred stain on the ground.

Ponting could see no buildings; nothing more than crumbled mounds of rubble.

"Holy Mary," a soldier gasped in a whisper of incredulity. "It's gone, man. The whole fuckin' village has been destroyed."

In the ear-ringing aftermath of the furious artillery barrage a new sound filled the sky. It was the whine of jet engines, approaching from the east and travelling fast. Ponting peered up through the haze of billowing smoke.

"Air attack!"

A formation of four Russian Su-34 'Fullback' fighter bombers flashed high overhead, faint black dots in the sky that gradually took on menacing shape and form as they circled the remains of Becejty, then peeled off one-by-one to launch their attacks. The whine of their engines shivered the air as they swooped like birds of prey to unleash their deadly payload of bombs. The earth erupted in fresh fireball explosions and roiling columns of smoke that blotted out the light, turning the dawn sky into an eerie, evil twilight.

Ponting watched the air strike, appalled and stunned. The Su-34s formed up over the lake, then turned back east, passing directly overhead of Fort Suicide. Ponting watched them disappear beyond the horizon just as the sun began to rise, blood-red, into the smoke-filled sky.

As he continued to stare, stupefied by the abrupt unholy carnage the Russians had unleashed, the eastern skyline seemed to change shape. It was as if the earth had suddenly broken open and from within its dark depths had erupted something evil and ominous. Ponting stared with the binoculars pressed to his eyes for several long moments, his fear slithering in the pit of his guts as the darkened mass spread out across the entire landscape.

"Can you see anything, Lieutenant?" asked Harley.

"Still too far away to identify," Ponting muttered, "but there's movement, and it's coming towards us."

Sergeant Wagner cocked his ear towards the direction of the horizon. "Can you hear that?"

Ponting set down the glasses and listened. So did Sergeant Harley and the rest of the men nearby. It was the sound of a thousand faint squeaks and the dull unmistakable rumble of heavy engines. Wagner felt his mouth turn dry.

"Tanks and APCs," Harley said.

Ponting scanned the skyline again with the binoculars and this time the spreading dark mass across the rim of the world had enough shape and form for him to identify the individual components. It was a Battalion of Russian T-90s, still several miles away but closing at speed, their tracks kicking up a skirt of dust to smudge their approach. The Lieutenant set down the binoculars and peered at the pale faces of the men lined along the length of the deep trench.

"It's happening," he said, his voice strangely detached and awed with incredulity. "The Russians are attacking."

*

Ponting cried out to Private Skinner. The RTO came scrambling along the length of the crowded trench.

"Try to reach Company HQ," Ponting ordered in a frantic rush of words. "See if the Captain or any of the other officers have survived. Then get on to Battalion HQ. Tell the Lieutenant Colonel that we have the entire fucking Russian Army coming at us. Tell them the attack is at least Battalion strength, but probably greater. We need the Arty to prioritize our sector and be ready for TRPs. Understand?"

Skinner dashed away down the length of the trench, running for his radio. Ponting turned and stared at the pale faces of the men pressed close around, waiting for him to lead them. He felt the burden of responsibility like a leaden weight. What he decided next would determine if many of these men died or survived.

All the training, planning and preparation of the COP's defenses was over. There was nothing left to do but fight like the devil.

"Get to your positions and keep your heads down!" he cupped his hands to his mouth and called, his voice carrying to every corner of the compound. "As soon as the Russians are in range, we hit the bastards with everything we've got!"

*

The lead Battalion of Russian T-90 tanks crashed across the Polish border and rumbled towards Szelment in three lines with about a hundred meters between each tank. As they descended the gentle slope and reached the wide pan of the valley, the formation became ragged as some tanks leaped eagerly ahead of the rest. Once the first tanks reached the outskirts of the village, a line of BMP-2 armored personnel carriers appeared. The APCs crested the skyline, seemed to pause for a heartbeat, and then followed the T-90s down the slope. In the strengthening light of the new dawning day the entire horizon became filled with surging Russian armor.

Suddenly the forest that had concealed the advance enemy force of tanks and APCs erupted with a howl of roaring noise and movement. More tanks and more enemy BMP-2s swarmed from the dense stand of woods in a tight column, snaking north once they cleared the tree line and making for a road that skirted the rim of the valley and ran directly towards the ruins of Becejty.

Guy Ponting watched the approaching storm of enemy armor and felt the insects of his fear crawl along the flesh of his arms. For a moment he stared, stunned and debilitated by sheer disbelief, as his mouth turned dry and a cold sweat of foreboding washed over him. RTO Skinner came splashing through the mud, carrying a hand-held radio. He was red-faced with panic and breathing hard. His eyes looked wild and hectic.

"Can't raise Company HQ, Lieutenant. The line to Becejty is dead," Skinner blurted. "I got on to Battalion but it's a madhouse. From what I could make out on the radio, the Russians are attacking along a ten-mile wide front. A German

Bundeswehr Company four clicks to our north just reported contact with a Russian Battalion of T-72s supported by motorized infantry."

Ponting nodded grimly, trying to visualize the tactical situation. He was about to give Skinner a new radio message to relay when the skyline east of the COP suddenly lit up with a hellish glow of flickering red light.

"Take cover!" Sergeant Harley's voice boomed.

A moment later the air overhead filled with the shriek of incoming artillery fire and the world turned ominously dark.

The first Russian artillery rounds landed on the forward-facing slope of the outpost, tearing apart the earthen rampart and showering the men in their trenches with clods of mud and flung rocks. One round left a crater ten yards wide in the soft dirt and shook the ground so that, to the men cowering deep in their trenches, it felt like the aftershock of an earthquake. The monstrous roar of the explosion filled the air with grey swirling smoke. Then the rounds began to fall like a relentless downpour of rain, pummeling the knoll with a succession of mighty hammer-blows.

One round landed on the tangled perimeter wall of C-wire and cleaved open a five-yard-wide breach in the flimsy barricade. Another exploded next to the Humvee, destroying the vehicle in an oily ball of fire. Two rounds landed close to the sandbagged wall that protected the outpost's forward-facing trench where Ponting and most of the Platoon crouched in cover. Fragments of whistling metal thwacked into the bags, tearing some open and heaving others down into the muddy trench.

The artillery barrage became an unending thunder of noise and whistling death that had to be endured. Again, and again explosions rattled across the exposed parade ground. The watchtower took a direct hit and exploded in a hail of fire and death. Both of the men manning the heavy machine gun position were immolated by the searing fireball. The tower collapsed in a blast of shattered debris and crashed to the ground, sandbags, wooden posts and mangled body parts flung a hundred meters in every direction.

"Christ!" Guy Ponting flinched and peered cautiously above the eyeline of the sandbagged trench to where the watchtower had stood. All that remained of the fortification was a smoking hole of churned earth. A splintered piece of timber landed in the trench at his feet, still smoldering. Another round landed in the middle of the compound and the ground was heaved up in a flash of flames and smoke, the violence of the blast so fierce that it rattled his teeth. The sound of the explosion rang like a thunderclap. Ponting turned in a deafened daze and peered down into the smoke-filled valley. The closest Russian tanks were passing the ruins of Postawelek and closing on their position behind drifting skeins of oily haze.

As quickly as the thunder of the massed Russian artillery bombardment began, it ended with equal abruptness. The eerie silence that followed was not a true silence, for the floor of the valley was swarming with advancing Russian armor, their engines howling as they surged towards the knoll – yet to the Americans standing at their posts deep in their trenches, it seemed like a blessed moment of respite.

The soldiers lifted their heads warily, their ears ringing, their senses numbed, and peered with red-rimmed eyes at the fresh hell spread out across the landscape before them. The closest Russian tanks were less than two kilometers away, crossing the churned ground that had been upheaved when Postawelek had been pounded to rubble. Ponting saw the lead enemy tanks dipping and climbing through deep shell craters, the drab steel beasts pitching like they were boats on a storm-tossed ocean.

"Everyone to their places!" Ponting ordered.

The men manning the heavy weapons scrambled from the shelter of the deep trench and scurried, bent-double, towards their firing positions.

"Get those Javelins ready for action!" Ponting barked, then turned and looked through the press of jostling bodies around him to locate the RTO. "Skinner. Get the Battalion's Arty on the line and tell them to stand by for a fire mission."

The waiting was over. The Russian attack was coming. Now it was time for the Americans to fight back.

Ponting drew a deep breath and took another long look at the approaching enemy armor. His instinct told him something wasn't right. He frowned, puzzled, and was suddenly overcome by a sense of disconcerted confusion.

The Russian tanks at the vanguard of the assault seemed to be slowing down…

*

The forward observer lay concealed at the edge of the forest, his position well camouflaged on a gentle rise of tree-covered grass. The Russian officer peered at the knoll of cratered ground in the smoke-obscured distance for several seconds through his binoculars then reached for his radio.

"The Americans are moving into positions to repel the attack," he muttered. "I can see men rushing about the compound."

Six miles behind the Russian armored advance, and located in a clearing on the Lithuanian side of the border, the massed guns of the Russian artillery batteries were reloaded and awaiting fresh orders. The Russian Colonel in command of a battery of 2S7 Pion self-propelled 203mm heavy artillery pieces checked the stopwatch in his hand and looked questioningly at his Lieutenant.

"Do you have confirmation from the OP?"

The Lieutenant shook his head and clamped his hands over the headset he wore to block out the sounds of idling engines. He frowned in concentration, listening to a relayed message, then nodded his head. He snatched the headset off and raised a green flag. The Colonel smiled mirthlessly and passed the order to his battery commander.

"Fire! Three rounds."

The Pion entered service with the Soviet Army in the late 1970s and remained in service with the present-day Russian and Belarusian militaries. It was regarded as the most powerful conventional artillery system in the world, designed to eliminate important enemy targets such as command bunkers. Fitted with a load assisting system, manned by a crew of fourteen, and capable of firing a one hundred and ten kilogram HE-FRAG projectile at targets almost fifty kilometers away, it was a monster of the battlefield.

The Pions were already loaded and awaiting orders. The sound of the six massive howitzers firing at the same time sent a shockwave across the ground that flattened the grass and shivered the air. As each gun fired, the vehicles sank down on their suspension and rocked against the spread steel legs of their supports, digging deep ruts into the ground.

The Colonel heard the wicked punch of each round through the heavy protection of his noise defenders and chuckled with malicious glee.

*

"Fuck!" Guy Ponting swore vehemently as the sound of approaching artillery rounds shrieked across the smoke-stained sky. He screamed at the top of his lungs. "For Christ's sake, get back down! Everybody get back into the main trench and take cover!"

He had ordered his men to their positions and they were now caught, cruelly exposed in the open. Ponting clenched his fists and cringed as the first of the Russian shells plunged down out of the clouds and began exploding.

Men began to die.

Sergeant Harley seized his young Lieutenant's collar and thrust his face close. His eyes were savage, his voice a cruel snarl. "You ain't got time for a fucking pity party, Lieutenant. It's fucking war. Men die. You do your fuckin' job to the best of your ability and you keep doing it until your dead. Understand? Every one of these men are counting on you!"

Harley pushed the ashen-faced Lieutenant aside and went running back along the trench, shouting for the men to find cover as the first Russian rounds began to explode across the compound. As he ran his face was turned up to the smoke darkened sky, watching the fall of the incoming artillery.

Suddenly the earth around them erupted. Sergeant Harley had never in all his years of warfare experienced anything like it. When the first Russian round landed in the center of the compound the ground seemed to dissolve and liquify – turned to dust in a storm of fire and thunder.

Several soldiers were caught in the open as the first incoming rounds exploded. One man had been running for the sandbagged shelter of a trench at the northwestern corner of the outpost where the Javelin anti-tank teams were sheltered. White-hot metal fragments caught the man in the back and slammed him, bleeding and screaming, face-first to the ground. He lay in the drifting dust and smoke, thrashing in agony, his flesh hacked and minced as though he had been fed through a grinder. A second, and then a third artillery round struck the compound before anyone could dash to the injured man's aid. He died in the dirt, the screams of his last agonized moments drowned out by the cataclysmic eruptions of the incoming Russian fire.

A Corporal on his way across the uneven ground to man one of the heavy machine guns was bowled over by the earth-shattering blast of an explosion. He staggered to his feet, winded and dazed, and then was immolated in the fireball as the next Russian round landed a few seconds later.

The clamorous thunder of the artillery barrage was a deafening roar that reached the point of pain. One soldier covered both his ears and sank down in the bottom of the deep trench, sobbing inconsolably.

Sergeant Harley watched the devastation from behind the sandbagged shelter of the trench, his face contorted as he continued to scream for men to find cover. Then an explosion landed on the forward slope of the knoll, lifting the Sergeant off his feet and hurling him to the ground. The earth shuddered like it was a living thing and the air filled with clouds of swirling dust and debris. Rocks and chunks of torn dirt fell like rain, knocking the breath from him, suffocating him in the choking fog. Part of the trench wall collapsed and for a moment the Sergeant was buried alive by the tons of avalanching dirt and mud.

Guy Ponting splashed through the mire and seized the Sergeant's arm, dragging the big man free. Harley's face was black with mud, and he was bleeding from a split lip. He spat out a mouthful of dirt and swore.

And still the Russian artillery continued to pound the outpost's perimeter.

Lieutenant Ponting found RTO Skinner cowering at the bottom of the main trench, covered in mud. The Private's hands were shaking as he knelt hunched over his radio. He looked up into Ponting's face and his eyes were crazed with fear.

"I can't… I can't…" he tried to work the radio with fumbling fingers. Skinner's face was a mud-streaked mask of panic. "I just can't…"

Ponting crouched down in the mud beside the Private and forced steel into his voice.

"You can, and you fucking will," the Lieutenant felt a fraud, for his terror was just as real as the Private's. But Sergeant Harley's cruel admonishment about leadership still echoed in his ears. He had to portray calm composure even though he felt sick with fear. "As soon as this artillery bombardment is over, the Russians are going to come storming across that valley and up the slope of the knoll. Without Arty support, we're all going to die. It's up to you, Skinner. Get the fucking radio working and get Battalion on the line."

It seemed to take a long moment for the Lieutenant's words to register with the RTO. He stared, not comprehending – and then nodded his head with a guilty jerk. The insanity of his terror receded from his eyes and he took a deep, shuddering breath to steady himself.

"Yes, sir."

"Good man," Ponting forced a tight smile. "And when you get through to Battalion, ask them why they aren't using a counter battery radar to track incoming rounds and taking out the Russian guns. We're getting fucking slaughtered up here, and Battalion is doing sweet-fuck-all to support us."

There seemed no pattern to the hail of artillery rounds exploding across the compound. Two explosions were separated by just a split-second, and then there was a delay of up to a minute before another round came screaming out of the sky. The unbearable clamor of noise and tense chaos frayed men's nerves and pounded their senses until they simply cringed in the mud and prayed for the nightmare to end.

Sergeant Davin Wagner heard a man groaning in agony and peered above the lip of the trench. The grounds of the compound were cratered and furrowed, the air furnace-hot and stinking of cordite and smoke. Through the drifting curtain of grey haze and dust he saw a man's leg and boot protruding from a tumble of slashed sandbags that had been blown apart by an explosion. The Sergeant called out to the man but the thunder of the artillery was overwhelming. Wagner gnawed his lip, then impulsively handed the man next to him his M4. He scrambled up the muddy slope of the trench and then began slithering like a snake across the broken ground. An explosion at the southeast corner of the outpost flung an avalanche of dirt across his back and shoulders. He ducked his head and waited for the earth beneath him to stop trembling, then moved on. When he reached the buried body, he was gasping for air; his lungs on fire and his face lathered in sweat. He tugged at the boot and called out, shouting above the storm of explosions.

The boot moved in his hand. He tugged again, harder, and the leg moved.

"Can you hear me, soldier? Can you hear me?"

Wagner pushed at the sandbag covering the man's leg and recoiled in sudden gasping horror. The limb had been severed from the body six inches above the knee, amputated cleanly by the slash of flying metal fragments. Wagner clutched the dead bleeding stump of flesh in his hand and felt the gorge rise into the back of his throat. He scrabbled away, his hands wet with blood, an involuntary sob of shock in the back of his throat.

He turned on his stomach and crawled back for the trench just as the last Russian shell left the barrel of its Pion howitzer and shrieked into the sky, rising high into the air on a trajectory for the COP. As the round reached the zenith of its arc and began to whistle through the air towards the American compound, Sergeant Wagner heard the ominous sound of its approach and knew, with some fatalistic intuition, that death was approaching. He was just a few yards from the safety of the deep trench when the Russian round landed near the ruins of the watchtower, gouging a massive crater from the earth as it erupted in a fireball of flames and fragments.

The quake of the massive explosion forced the soldiers to duck deep into the trench for cover. When they rose again into the smoke-drifting aftermath, they saw Sergeant Wagner's broken body, so bloodily beaten by the blast that it was barely recognizable. His head had been severed, the uniform torn and hanging in smoldering tatters from his remains. He had been struck by over a hundred steel fragments. One of the men gagged then retched over his boots.

In the stunned, eerie silence that followed the explosion a single voice cried out, aghast with fear and foreboding.

"The Russian tanks are advancing again!"

"Everyone to their positions!"

Chapter 7:

Ponting left the defense of the main trench in the hands of Sergeant Harley and scampered to the northwest corner of the COP where the Platoon's two Javelin anti-tank teams were cowered in separate sandbagged trenches. As he dashed across the shell-cratered ground, he turned his head to gauge the Russian advance across the valley. A dozen T-90 tanks were visible through the drifting smoke, though he knew there were many more concealed behind the blanket of haze. The closest Russian MBT was accelerating across a narrow irrigation ditch, marked by a lush green line in the farm fields about a kilometer and a half from the knoll.

Ponting flung himself down into the shelter of the closest trench, gasping.

The position was reinforced with sandbags and lengths of timber, shielded on the inside by thin sheets of iron plating. There were two men in the cramped space and a stockpile of six missile tubes in their cannisters.

Due to the depth of the trench, the Javelin's operator was standing with his weight forward, his legs spaced and braced, the command launch unit set on his right shoulder and a missile already loaded. His teammate stood off to the side holding a second missile cylinder by its carry handle, ready to reload.

The two men were covered in mud and dirt, their faces streaked with runnels of sweat. The operator had his eye pressed to the Javelin's viewing lens, the cumbersome fifty-pound weight of the system balanced evenly.

Ponting watched while the soldier scanned the approaching Russian T-90s and acquired a target. He locked the infra-red seeker.

"Hit the bastards!" Ponting's voice was savage.

The operator pulled the trigger and the missile leaped from the launcher in 'soft' launch to minimize back blast and to conceal their firing position. Once in the air, the missile's main rocket motor activated and sent the projectile lancing into the sky.

The Javelin was a fire-and-forget anti-tank weapon; the operator slid the unit from his shoulder and the support man beside him immediately began to reload with a fresh missile. Ponting watched the Javelin missile skid through the air and then climb high over the battlefield on a streaking tail of white smoke. When it reached the zenith of its trajectory, it turned over in the clouds and began to plunge to earth, homing in on its unsuspecting target.

Down in the valley the lead Russian T-90 tank jounced over a small rise, its engine belching black smoke, its steel tracks gouging the rain-softened farm fields. Then suddenly it exploded in a huge fireball of roiling orange flame. A second later the vehicle was consumed in a cloud of smoke as the steel carcass was torn apart by the Javelin. The projectile ripped through the vehicle's thin top turret armor and blew the tank into a thousand metal pieces.

"Hit!" Ponting exulted, and felt the cruel savage thrill of retribution. "Keep firing!"

The Javelin was reloaded and the operator hoisted the cumbersome CLU back onto his shoulder. His support man thrust a pointed finger through the smoke, indicating at T-90 swerving diagonally around a small stand of trees as it closed on the knoll. The operator bent his head forward and patiently sighted the tank through the viewing lens.

A second Javelin missile launched into the sky with a *'whoosh'* of expelled back blast and hunted across clouds, the infra-red seeker guiding the projectile on its way. At the top of its climb above the battlefield, thrusters corrected the weapon's course, guiding it unerringly towards its target.

'Boom!'

The thundering rumble of the second T-90 exploding carried to the men around Fort Suicide a split-second after the enemy tank erupted in flames and smoke. Flying shards of ragged iron flew into the air and a thick black column of oily smoke climbed into the sky.

Around the outpost, the men in the forward-facing trench gave a ragged little cheer of brave defiance.

"Keep firing!" Ponting clapped the operator on the shoulder and scampered to the adjoining trench, fifteen paces away. As he ran, a Russian mortar shell suddenly whistled through the air and landed a hundred yards beyond the COP's perimeter. The sound of the explosion was trivial compared to the earth-shattering thunder of the massed Russian artillery the Platoon had endured. Ponting gave the mortar fire a dismissive, contemptuous glance as he slid down into the new trench – and into fumbling confusion.

The support man in the dugout was on his knees, trying desperately to remove a Javelin missile from its canister while nursing a broken arm. The man had his sleeve rolled up to his forearm and Ponting could see an inch of shattered bone protruding through the thin flesh that covered the point of the soldier's elbow. His lower arm and hand were streaked with runnels of bright red blood and caked in mud.

Ponting turned and bellowed across the compound for Sergeant Harley to send a replacement, then helped the injured man load the Javelin. The soldier was white-faced and swaying on his feet, shivering against shock. His features were wrenched into a grimace of pain as, together, the two men fitted the missile into the CLU. The operator seized the bulky contraption and hoisted it onto his shoulder. Ponting pushed the injured man down onto the ground as the operator locked on to a target and pulled the trigger.

The CLU recoiled against the operator's shoulder as the Javelin streaked away across the valley, then went into its lethal climb.

For a moment Ponting lost sight of the missile as it disappeared behind a curtain of oily black smoke. Two seconds later he saw a small white streak, glowing like a flare, as it plunged down onto a Russian tank. The T-90 was about a kilometer away, just emerging from a haze of smoke and drifting diesel exhaust, when the Javelin struck. It seemed to Ponting that the tank shuddered at the instant of impact, then blew apart. The fireball of the explosion consumed the

Russian tank and then the fire dissolved into a tower of black boiling smoke.

The Javelin operator gave a snarling whoop of triumph.

A red-faced Private and a medic appeared at the edge of the trench. The medic helped haul the injured man out of the muddy ditch and the mud-covered Private jumped down to take his place. He was a broad-shouldered brawny young man from the Midwest with straw-colored hair and the physique of a running back. He hefted a new missile cylinder from the stockpile at the rear of the trench and loaded it quickly.

Ponting pointed down the slope to a T-90 that was pulling ahead of the Russian formation, the vehicle swaying on its suspension as it crashed through a ploughed field of young corn stalks, throwing up a trail of flung mud from its tracks. As Ponting singled out the tank, the vehicle suddenly fired several smoke canisters and disappeared behind the brown haze. Ponting snarled.

"Take that bastard out," he ordered. Now the Russian guns had fallen silent and the fighting was imminent, Ponting suddenly wanted the Russians to come. He felt consumed by a reckless rage. He wanted to strike back; to inflict as much destruction on the enemy as was possible. He felt he had a score to settle and a point to prove to himself, his men, and to the Russians.

Sergeant Harley, waiting in the main trench with the bulk of the Platoon's survivors, walked along the fire step, talking quietly to each and every soldier standing at the sandbags, ready to open fire. One of the men flinched when a T-90 down in the valley that had begun firing smoke cannisters suddenly exploded in a huge eruption of flames.

"Get yourself right to fight, soldier," Harley shoved his face close to the man, his expression ferocious.

The Sergeant walked on, reached the end of the trench and began to return, never once looking at the Russian advance, keeping his steps calm and measured. He did it so the men could see that he was unconcerned; he did it for morale – even though his heart thumped like a drum in his chest and his hands were cold and clammy with sweat. One of the Russian tanks fired a HEAT round that sailed high overhead and exploded two hundred meters beyond the perimeter. A second tank opened fire. The round went howling high and exploded harmlessly in dead ground. Sergeant Harley turned at last and gave the Russian advance a contemptuous, disdainful glare.

"Fucking Russians can't shoot straight," he sneered. "Reckon they're raw troops just come from sucking their momma's tits, boys," his expression turned suddenly wolfish and he raised his voice. "So, let's show them how Americans fight. Let's send them all back to Moscow in body bags!"

*

The Russian tanks closest to the knoll suddenly turned northwest to bypass the American COP and began firing smoke cannisters to conceal their maneuver. The valley floor became smothered in thick swirls of white and brown haze.

Lieutenant Ponting climbed cautiously out of the heavy weapons trench and went forward to the perimeter wire at a crouch. He peered at the Russian advance, trying to understand the enemy's plan. Through the shifting clouds of smoke, the T-90s in the vanguard of the assault were forming into ragged columns and steering towards the road that bypassed the outpost and ran directly to the village of Becejty.

Ponting was joined by Sergeant Harley. The two men ducked down behind a wall of sandbags and peered through an embrasure. The Russian tanks were broadside to the compound and moving further away while the ranks of Russian troop carriers continued to advance directly towards them.

"What are the bastards up to?" Ponting frowned.

"The tanks in the valley are moving to link up with the advance column we found in the forest. They're going to drive through the gap in our lines and go straight for Becejty."

"Cutting us off from reinforcements," Ponting realized.

"Yes."

"And breaking through our lines. Christ! Once the Russians have armored units in our rear, they'll threaten the entire line all the way north to the Kaliningrad border."

"In which case we're fucked," the Sergeant added dryly.

Both men ducked as a Russian tank turned its turret towards the outpost and fired a HEAT round. They saw the puff of smoke bloom beyond the barrel then heard the wicked whine of the incoming round. It landed on the edge of the helicopter LZ.

Ponting continued to stare at the maneuvering tanks. He shouted out to his Javelin teams. "Hit those enemy tanks at the head of the column," he pointed to the road that bypassed their position.

"Lieutenant, what about the APCs?" Harley protested. "Any minute now we're going to be facing twenty armored vehicles and upward of two hundred enemy infantry. Those tanks are no longer our fight. They're someone else's battle now. Our war is right in front of us."

"I know," Ponting snapped, tortured by a terrible choice. If he directed fire against the advancing Russian tanks that threatened to punch clear through the Allied line, the COP would be overrun by Russian infantry. But if he ignored the menace of the tanks and directed the Javelin teams to concentrate on the swarm of BMP-2s that were approaching the foot of the knoll, the enemy T-90s would overrun Becejty and cut the Platoon off from reinforcements.

Ponting bit his lip, assailed by bleak doubts and caught in the snare of a diabolical dilemma with no right decision, and with time against him.

From the length of the main trench came the sounds of men preparing their weapons and readying themselves to face the Russian infantry. The first of the enemy's armored personnel carriers crossed a green grassy line that marked an irrigation ditch. They were less than a thousand yards away. One man lifted his voice above the distant rumble of the Russian vehicles and began reciting passages from the Bible. Sergeant Harley turned and snarled at the soldier.

"Private Sandford! Shut your fucking mouth, boy, or I'll personally arrange an appointment with God for you." Private Sandford fell sullenly silent. In his place, the turret-mounted 30mm autocannons atop the approaching Russian BMP-2s suddenly opened fire.

The sound of hammering death was a fierce ripping noise. Bullets whipped the churned ground along the facing slope of the knoll and slapped into the wall of sandbags that lined the top of the trench. Each strike was like a heavy punch that flailed and shredded the redoubt, forcing the Americans along the perimeter to shrink down into cover.

Ponting tucked his head between his knees just as a flurry of bullets thudded into the ground in front of him. Clods of dirt and a churned cloud of dust filled the air. The thrashing flail of Russian fire seemed to last an eternity. When at last an eerie breath of silence fell across the outpost, he eased his head above the sandbags and blinked into the thick swirling dust.

The Russian APCs were gathering around the foot of the slope, pulling to a halt to disgorge their cargoes of infantry.

"Time's up, Lieutenant," Sergeant Harley drew his M4 and aimed through an embrasure at the closest Russian troop carrier. "We live or die on your orders."

Ponting shook his head. His mouth felt as dry as a desert. Then, quite suddenly, he found a third option.

He turned back to the Javelin teams and cupped his hands to his mouth. "Open fire on the tanks driving towards Becejty. Hit the head of the column and slow them down." Then he bellowed for RTO Skinner, suddenly seized by a wild glimmer of desperate hope. Skinner came scrambling through the dust and dirt, crawling on his stomach with the radio strapped to his back. He slithered into the ditch beside the Lieutenant, filthy and sweating.

"Get Battalion on the line. I need close air support right now."

Skinner unstrapped the radio and set up in the bottom of the trench. His voice was shaky with panic as he blurted the Lieutenant's orders through a hiss of wavering static. It took thirty seconds for the call to be re-routed to a JTAC (Joint Terminal Attack Controller) aboard an AWACS circling ninety miles behind the battlefront.

Skinner handed the Lieutenant the radio phone and Ponting cupped his free hand to his ear to isolate the radio messages as a pair of A-10 Warthogs fifteen nautical miles east of Warsaw responded to the urgent 'All Players' call.

"Recoil Sixteen, Badman Sixty-One, copy. Standby for AO update." Ponting heard the JTAC coordinating with the A-10s.

Ponting spat dirt from his mouth as the radio hissed open-line static and he was connected directly to the aircraft's pilots.

"Recoil Sixteen, Badman Sixty-One, AO update. We are a Platoon of American infantry fifteen hundred meters northeast of Becejty at Combat Outpost Bravo Zero-Six. We are under attack from a Battalion-strength force of Russian T-90 tanks and at least two Battalions of supporting BMP-2 troop carriers. Say when ready Nine-Line."

"Ready Nine-Line," the pilot commanding the lead Warthog sounded calm and detached.

Ponting went through the 9-Line procedure quickly, giving the pilots the target grid coordinates and the keypad number, then cleared the A-10s 'hot' to attack. The pilot commanding the two-ship flight acknowledged the instructions.

"ETA ninety seconds. Standby."

Ponting threw down the radio and stole a glance over the lip of the sandbagged barricade. Down on the valley's floor, near the foot of the knoll and not more than three hundred meters from where he crouched, a dozen Russian BMP-2s were slewing to a halt in the grassy mud. The vehicles rear doors crashed open and Russian infantry spilled into the smoke-filled morning. The enemy soldiers began to spread out, throwing themselves down into muddy furrows. It had been Russian troops like these who had conquered all of the Baltic States and Poland in just a few short savage months. Now they were attacking again, using overwhelming numbers and brute force to hammer their way once more to triumph.

The BMP-2s re-commenced firing at the crest of the slope, their autocannons throwing down a solid sheet of spitting lead. Then the first Russian infantry began to advance, moving up the incline of the muddy slope in short bounds. They advanced in a loose mass of bodies; running, kneeling to fire, then running again. One of the Russian soldiers knelt and aimed into the drifting smoke, putting a bullet within three inches of Ponting's face. He ducked down behind the sandbags and glanced at his watch, then to Sergeant Harley.

"Get back to the main trench and keep everyone's heads down. We've got two A-10s inbound, ETA now thirty-five seconds."

Harley grunted. "I hope this works, Lieutenant," he scrambled to the edge of the trench and prepared himself for the short dangerous dash across a no-man's land peppered with hot lead.

"As soon as the two A-10s clear the area, we give the Russians everything we've got," Ponting gave final instructions and then his voice turned reckless. "And if it doesn't work – I'll see you in Hell, Sergeant Harley."

The veteran Sergeant hesitated, then turned back, a wicked smile spreading across his mud-spattered face. "I'll be waiting at the gates for you, Lieutenant Ponting."

*

Four miles behind Allied lines, Lieutenant Colonel Chuck McCluskey, commander of the American infantry Battalion, burst in to the headquarters tent fuming with anger and waving a message flimsy in his hand.

"What the fuck is going on at the battlefront?" he demanded to know of his assembled staff. The tent was a chaos of raised voices, incoming radio chatter and activity bordering on panic. "I've got reports Becejty has been shelled and another report from an outpost northeast of the village claiming they are under attack from several Battalions of Russian armor and APCs!" McCluskey glared across the small space and locked his eyes on his S2 intelligence officer. He fixed the man with a baleful glare. "Someone tell me what the fuck is going on, right now!"

The Lieutenant Colonel's hair was tousled, and he had dressed in a hurry, shaken from his sleep by an aide. His eyes were red and puffy, his features sagged by age and endless stress. A low-level functionary put a steaming mug of coffee in his hand and he glared around the confined space of the tent as he drank.

"Well?" he bellowed.

Major Wayland Young, the S2 who had interviewed Guy Ponting in his hospital bed, felt the blood drain from his face and a sudden sense of sickening vertigo. He tried to hold the Lieutenant Colonel's fearsome glare, but his gaze wavered and flicked guiltily to a large map of northern Poland that was spread across a table. Lieutenant Colonel McCluskey closed in on the man.

"Young, it's your job to know what's going on with the enemy in front of us. How could you not have had any warning that *at least a full Division of enemy armor* was massing on the Lithuanian border?"

The S2 withered under the blowtorch of the Lieutenant Colonel's furious glare. "There… there was one report, sir," Young balked. "It came from the new Lieutenant at COP Bravo Zero-Six. But his information was regarded as dubious and the decision was made to discard it."

"*Discard* it?" McCluskey seized on the word and the rage misted red in his eyes. "By who?"

"It was Captain Anson from Army Intelligence's decision," Young lied to protect himself. His voice cracked and rose an octave. "He felt the Lieutenant's report lacked credibility, as did the Lieutenant's Company commander, Captain Gatfield," the man stammered.

The Lieutenant Colonel wheeled on the functionary who had fetched him coffee. "Find Gatfield, and get a hold of this Captain Anson from Army Intelligence," the Battalion commander snarled. "I'll have someone's guts ripped out for this fuck up."

The junior officer scurried out through the opening of the tent and disappeared. Lieutenant Colonel McCluskey stared after the man for a long moment, trying to put a lid on his rage that threatened to boil over. He clenched his fist and pounded the top of the map table in frustration, then pressed his lips into a thin bloodless line as he stared down at the map. He turned to a radio operator. "Get Brigade on the line and tell them I need men and armor reinforcements before the entire Allied front collapses and the Army gets pushed all the way back to Warsaw."

*

It was a sound so faint and so elusive that for long seconds Guy Ponting didn't trust his ears. He cocked his head to one side and closed his eyes. The whine seemed to waver on the air. He turned and peered west; searching the smoke-stained sky. He could see nothing… and yet the sound persisted beneath the louder, closer overlays of Russian tank and APC engines, and the incessant snarl of enemy machine gun fire.

Ponting frowned. The sound rose and then faded. Then the thick curtain of smoke was shredded by a gust of breeze and Ponting saw two black dots, skimming the horizon, still far away but coming closer with every passing second.

The two A-10 Thunderbolts arrived over the battlefront from the west, then banked south and flew a wide circuit to approach the target grid reference on a south-to-north attacking run. The planes were concealed behind layers of drifting smoke and flew a terrain-masking route, using valleys, gentle hills and the clumped patches of forest to hide their approach.

The Warthogs were mean brutes of the battlefield; unlovely looking close-support aircraft armed with the world's most powerful forward-firing aircraft-mounted gun thrusting from its snout and fitted with thick Hershey-bar shaped wings that could carry an assortment of bombs, rockets and missiles to the enemy.

It was slow through the air but savage in attack.

The two Hog drivers came hunting across the grassy plateau and then swooped down into the shallow valley, both pilots concentrating fiercely in the high-workload environment that demanded their complete concentration. Enclosed in a 'bathtub' of titanium armor that surrounded the cockpits and a front windshield panel that was made of bullet-resistant glass so thick it could take a direct hit from a twenty-three-millimeter round, the lead Warthog lined up on the leading Russian APCs with his wingman flying a mile directly astern in the 'slot'.

Below them the entire valley floor was a chaos of moving enemy vehicles, smoke, flashing explosions and streaks of tracer fire that criss-crossed the battlefield.

The lead Hog driver put his aircraft's nose down and maneuvered across the valley at subsonic speed, flicking his eyes to the small round screen of the aircraft's onboard RWR (Radar Warning Receiver) as he made his final approach to target. The RWR showed no active SAM threats, but as a precaution he fired off flares and chaff, then double-checked his ECM (electronic countermeasures) pod was activated.

The Warthogs were each carrying a full drum of 30mm ammunition for their GAU-8 Avenger rotary cannon and six Maverick AGM-65 missiles.

The lead Warthog steered onto a cluster of BMP-2s that were stationery on the valley floor, just three hundred meters east of Bravo Zero-Six. The pilot counted a dozen enemy troop carriers and saw hundreds of Russian soldiers at the foot of the rise, beginning to ascend the slope. He put his aircraft into a shallow dive and lined up the target using the fixed gun pipper. He squeezed the trigger to its first detent, then calmly increased finger pressure. For a split-second nothing happened – and then the aircraft seemed to shake itself apart and all hell broke loose.

A deep roar of noise swamped the cockpit as the aircraft rumbled and shuddered like a buzzsaw. The front of the Warthog disappeared behind a juddering cloud of smoke as the stench of cordite filled the cockpit. The sledge-hammer roar of the GAU-8 seemed to still the battlefield. Then the sound was replaced by the deeper bass rumble of explosions as four of the Russian troop carriers erupted in fireballs of flame. The Warthog flew through the rising columns of black boiling smoke and emerged on the other side into clear air. It flashed over a line of T-90 tanks that were ascending the rim of the valley and forming up on a road.

The pilot continued to egress northwards until he was three miles beyond the valley, still flying low to avoid Russian mobile SAM sites. He put the Warthog into a slow lazy turn to the west and twisted his head round in the snug confines of the cockpit to watch the strafing run of his wingman.

The Hog driver in the trailing A-10 took his lead from the first Warthog and jinked his aircraft a little to the right to line up the same cluster of Russian BMP-2s at the foot of the slope. The grass around the destroyed vehicles was on fire, and he could see a dozen or more dead Russian soldiers strewn grotesquely across the ground. The four APCs were smoldering wrecks. Two were still burning fiercely, and the other two were blackened twisted shells trailing oily smoke into the sky. His eyes danced around the cockpit, moving from his RWR to his air speed indicator and then to check his dive angle. One of the BMP-2 troop carriers turned its turret and opened fire on the approaching aircraft. A liquid trail of white tracer fire whizzed past the Warthog's right wing.

From the cockpit the snarl of BMP-2s appeared as nothing more than tiny elongated shapes, like children's toys left scattered after play. The pilot zeroed in on a group of three Russian vehicles and flew the HUD pipper over the targets. He trimmed out the controls and then squeezed the trigger.

The mighty GAU-8 Avenger rotary cannon roared to life and the targets beyond the nose of the Warthog's rounded snout dissolved into a mist of churned earth, then smoke and fire. All three of the BMP-2s were struck and destroyed, two of them exploding in fireballs of bright orange flame. More Russian infantry were dead; some decimated by 30mm rounds and others hit with flying fragments from the exploding vehicles. The Warthog swept overhead like an angel of death and disappeared into the distance.

From his position behind the sandbags that lined the northwest corner of Fort Suicide, Lieutenant Ponting watched the two A-10s as they swept the valley's floor with a hail of death and fire. He had the radio receiver close to his ear as the two aircraft flash past his position.

"Delta Hotel!" he exalted with savage satisfaction. "Delta Hotel! Direct hit. Recoil Sixteen, hit the bastards again!"

"Negative Bravo Zero-Six, we're Bingo fuel and RTB," the pilot commanding the lead Warthog said through a hiss of radio static. His voice sounded detached and scrubbed of all emotion. "We'll see if we can rustle up some other players to join the party. Standby and good luck."

Ponting cursed under his breath and tossed the radio to RTO Skinner. "Keep monitoring the radio and don't fucking move. Let me know the moment you hear anything about more incoming air support."

The CAS attack had bought them time and a few seconds of breathing space.

Now the Platoon would need to fight for their lives.

Chapter 8:

Lieutenant Ponting braced himself like a sprinter at the starting blocks, and then made a scrambling dash from the heavy weapons bunker to the main trench. Russian machine gun fire stitched the ground at his feet and whistled past his face as he ran. The air seemed filled with the ghastly sounds of death and the fear rose in him; fear that he would die bleeding in the dirt. He dived head-first into the yawning dark hole of the main trench and fell hard against the fire step.

"Jesus!" He was shaken and breathing hard.

Sergeant Harley reached down a huge hand and hauled the Lieutenant to his feet. The troops defending the trench were all hunched down below the rim of the sandbags, their faces fraught with tension bordering on terror. Beyond the dark deep hole where they crouched, the Russian machine guns were in a fury. A torrent of hammering metal was being poured onto the ridge from the BMP-2s in the valley so that the air seemed to hum and tremble and the ground pulsed and heaved.

Guy Ponting took a deep breath. "Everyone to an embrasure!" His voice sounded weak and tremulous, but the Platoon had been anticipating the order.

Reluctantly at first, then with grim fatalistic resolve, the men in the trench stepped up onto the fire step and into the face of the maelstrom. The air was so heated and so thick with smoke that it was like stepping into a furnace. All along the COP's perimeter the men found firing positions, the barrels of their M4s thrust through gaps in the sandbags. One moment the crest of the knoll appeared deserted and the next it was bristling with American automatic weapons.

"Make the first few seconds count!"

The closest Russian infantry were half-way up the grassy slope, slipping in mud, stumbling in their fear, but still coming on; still looming closer to the barbed wire perimeter. Some of the enemy soldiers saw the Americans move into position along the ragged line of sandbags and threw themselves down into the dirt, anticipating the lethal volley that must soon come. Others dropped down to one knee and sprayed the crest of the knoll with automatic fire from their AK-74s. The Russian officers leading the assault urged their men on, cajoling, swearing; bellowing the need for urgency.

The heavy autocannon fire from the BMP-2s finally withered and was choked off as the Russian infantry rose higher up the face of the knoll. For a heartbeat an eerie silence fell over the battlefield. Guy Ponting's roaring voice shattered the stillness.

"Fire!"

Two dozen M4s fired at the same instant, hammering the air with payback for all the American Platoon had been forced to suffer and endure. For three solid seconds the lower slope of the knoll was washed in a sheet of chattering death before the fusillade became ragged as men reloaded and others scoured the muddy grass for fresh targets.

A handful of Russian infantry went down in the first furious moments of the firefight. A Russian Sergeant was shot flush in the mouth as he cried out a defiant challenge. He fell dead to the ground, the contents of his shattered skull splashing the man behind him with gore. Another Russian took four hits to the body and crumpled at the knees, dead before he hit the ground. A Russian Lieutenant was shot in the hand and the neck. He sagged sideways, a look of utter bewilderment on his face. For a moment he tottered to keep his balance, then stiffened and fell backwards, bright red blood staining the trampled grass.

"Keep firing!" Ponting shouted.

The Americans took to the task with cruel savagery. Since dawn they had cowered in the gloom, and endured an endless nightmare of explosions and shrapnel. They had cursed and swore and entreated their God to spare them. They had sobbed and stifled their terror. Now they wanted revenge.

For a heartbeat the Russian wave of advancing infantry wavered, daunted by the prospect of charging into the face of such fury. A Russian officer ran on until he realized he was alone near the top of the crest. He glanced back over his shoulder and saw his men down in the mud, firing blindly with panic.

"Follow me! Follow me!" the officer waved his arm and shouted. A dozen Russians sprinted forward, attempting to shorten the range and then overwhelm the Americans. Sergeant Harley shot the Russian officer in the head, then swung his M4 in an arc and picked off three of the following soldiers. Two of them died outright. The third man fell to the ground clutching at his thigh and screaming in shrill agony.

The whole valley seemed to echo with the relentless chattering hammer of automatic weapons fire, the American M4 and the Russian AK-74 so similar in sound that it was impossible to tell which troops had the ascendency. The slope of the knoll became smudged with grey swirling smoke that drifted and melded and was twitched by gunfire.

Guy Ponting shuffled along the trench with a clutch of spare magazines. He climbed up onto the firing step and clapped a man on the shoulder. The sound of the firefight and the criss-cross of bullets thrashing the air was a deafening maelstrom that hammered his ears, forcing him to shout to be heard.

"Gomez, there's a Russian officer to the left. He's taken cover in that shell crater. I want the bastard dead."

He moved on, his guts churning with fear and his breathing strained – yet outwardly he appeared calm. He reached Sergeant Harley who had positioned himself in the middle of the line. The veteran soldier saw the young Lieutenant's bloodless face and noted the nervous twitch that tugged at the muscles in his cheek, but said nothing.

Amongst the Russian troops swarming up the slope were half-a-dozen men carrying green flags. The flags were bright little patches of color on wooden shafts. Sergeant Harley saw one of the flag-bearers scrambling through a churned patch of furrowed mud and shot him in the head. The soldier's dead body tumbled backwards into the mire and the flag fluttered to the ground. Another Russian picked up the flag and ran forward a few blundering paces before he too was shot and killed.

"What are the flags for?" Ponting noticed the Sergeant's grim determination as he hunted the men carrying the bright banners.

"The Russians use them to measure the progress of the attack," Harley explained. "It's how their OPs know when to call off artillery fire, overwatch machine gun fire, or mortar support."

Ponting ran his eyes across the lower slope and saw three more similar flag carriers. The colors were edging backwards.

"The first attack is wavering," Harley gave his assessment. He ran his experienced eye across the lower slope, noting the dozens of dead Russian bodies in the grass. "But there's more trouble brewing."

At the foot of the knoll the seven burning BMP-2s were still ablaze, the fire and smoke from the destroyed vehicles thickening. It looked like a giant cauldron behind which more Russian troop carriers marshalled and more infantry assembled, preparing, the Sergeant assumed, for a fresh assault.

A whistle blew three shrill blasts and the Russians still on the lower levels of the slope began to edge backwards, firing from the hip to cover their withdrawal. In their wake they left a litter of dead and dying in the sifted smoke. Some of the wounded cried out vainly for help. Some screamed in agony. Others moaned and wept pitifully. The air smelled of cordite and sweat and fear and blood.

"Cease fire!" Ponting cupped his hands to his mouth and cried the order. A last few American M4s spat venom and then the battlefield lapsed into a desultory stillness. In the eerie aftermath, Ponting re-positioned the Platoon SAWs to the ends of the main trench while men replenished empty magazines. One soldier had his helmet upended and resting on a sandbag, crammed full of M4 magazines and grenades like it was a giant bowl of candy.

"Anyone wounded?" the Sergeants of each squad went up and down the line checking every man. The soldiers were sweat-soaked. Their faces were barely recognizable behind masks of dirt and grime. The two Javelin crews had almost exhausted their stockpile of missiles smashing the head of the T-90 column on the rim of the valley. Eight T-90s were shattered, smoking ruins, but now there were only a handful of the lethal missiles left to fire. The surviving Russian tanks moved west along the road trailing a rooster-tail of dust to mark their progress. Ponting watched the tanks with dark foreboding, knowing that he was seeing his Platoon's own inevitable destruction. Once the Russian armor seized the ruins of Becejty, Fort Suicide would effectively be cut off from reinforcements.

He put the fatalistic thought out of his mind and turned his attention back to the fight in front of him. Through the wall of smoke that shrouded the valley floor, he could see several hundred more Russian infantry massing. The BMP-2 troop carriers were parked haphazardly across the muddy ground; the turrets of their autocannons all elevated and facing the crest of the knoll. Behind that wall of shielding armor, the infantry were separating into three distinct groups, each at least Company strength.

Guy Ponting scraped his hand across his brow and realized with a start of surprise, that he was no longer terrified. His fear had been replaced by a stoic resolve that left him calm and clear-minded.

"Next time they attack, they'll overwhelm us," Sergeant Harley said.

"Next time they come, we'll fire the Claymores," Ponting retorted.

*

Russian mortar platoons set up behind the shelter of the parked BMP-2s and prepared to open fire on the crest of the knoll. The six 82mm weapons were each served by a crew of four who worked with well-drilled efficiency. Ponting watched the bustle of movement through the shifting skeins of smoke and knew it presaged the beginning of yet another Russian attack.

The mortar rounds arced high into the air and plunged down across the cratered space of the outpost in a ragged series of explosions and fountains of earth that shook the ground. The noise above the trench became suddenly deafening as the Russians found their range, and the sound became a single thunderous roar that drummed across the sky. Flying shrapnel whipped past Ponting's cheek and whacked into a sandbag beside him with a sound like an axe splitting wood.

The Americans were forced back down into the dark gloom of the trench while from the lower slope they could hear the Russian infantry assembling, their voices intensifying to a savage roar as they began to charge the rise. For several minutes the barrage continued unabated. Suddenly the mortar fire stopped. In the American trench Ponting saw his men glancing at him nervously as he gingerly lifted his head above the sandbagged wall. At first, he saw nothing but a curtain of smoke and drifting dust; a cloud so thick that beyond it the sun appeared blood red in the morning sky. Along the rim of the lower slope, the smoke seemed to be moving as if struck through with darker shades. The shadows became the grey shapes of running men.

"Here they come!" Ponting cried, and the Americans rose stoically to the fire step once more and peered down at the fresh hell that was about to overwhelm them.

The Russian infantry charge seemed as inevitable as a tidal wave. There were hundreds of soldiers attacking in three long lines. They stretched from one smoke-smudged edge of the rising ground to the other, separated by a space of fifty meters from the line that followed. Ponting saw men with green banners clutched in their hands and officers waving their arms in frantic encouragement to the troops that followed. The smoke twitched and roiled as the Russians burst into the open.

It seemed impossible that the Americans could survive such a force.

The closest line to the crest became ragged as some soldiers charged boldly into the waiting guns and others slipped, fell or simply cringed away from the imminent fury.

Ponting watched the Russians come on until the closest enemy troops were within a hundred meters.

"Fire!"

The crest of the ridge erupted in a firestorm of lead that cut a swathe through the advancing Russians and staggered the line. In a few furious seconds the front rank of enemy troops was reduced to a horror of writhing bodies and dreadful moans. One of the Russian flag-bearers went down, his legs shot out from under him. He scrabbled in the mud, hands thrashing and a high-pitched keening wail of agony in the back of his throat. Another man snatched up the fallen banner and was shot before he could take a step. A second man seized the patch of green cloth and waved it high above his head like a rally cry to those that followed. The flag fell again, the man and the material riddled with bullets.

Still the Russians drove forward. The second line of infantry reached the first and ran past them, skirting the piles of dead and dying, slipping on blood and gore as the incline steepened. Some Russian officers tried to hold the line together, hoping they could hit home as a single overwhelming tide, but no voice could be heard in the maelstrom of lead and death.

One of Ponting's men watched a Russian officer skirting the southern edge of the slope, trailing a rag-tag group of enemy troops in his wake. He tracked the officer, sighting down the barrel of his M4 but before he could fire, he was hit through the left eye by a Russian infantryman firing from further down the slope. The impact snapped the man's head back on his neck and flung his corpse down into the bottom of the trench. Blood splattered the sandbags. The dead body twitched in the mud for several seconds before stilling.

A Corporal standing not ten feet from Ponting had one of his ears shot away. He screamed in pain, his face a mask of shock and agony. He clamped his hand over the wound and slumped down moaning and sobbing until Sergeant Harley brusquely told the man to stop his damn noise.

"The Claymores," Ponting prayed he had not waited too long to give the order. The Russians were still stubbornly advancing into the withering hail of automatic fire, more ranks advancing through the mist of smoke to thicken the relentless, grinding charge. "Go now!"

A torrent of metal was being poured against the ridge from the Russian infantry as they worked their way up the rise. They were coming forward in small groups now, the long line shattered and all semblance of organization lost.

Sergeant Harley slung his M4 over his shoulder and raced towards the southeast corner of the main trench where the Claymore clackers had been gathered. "Make a hole!" he shouted as he ran, dodging the wounded and dying. Bullets whipsawed about his ears. He was aware that the Platoon was beginning to take casualties. He saw two men unmoving in the bottom of the trench and several others were grimacing through the pain of their wounds.

He reached the M57 clackers at the end of the trench and took a last long look above the sandbags at the progress of the Russian advance.

There were six of the small triggering devices, hanging between two sandbags like a cluster of windchimes dangling from strings. Each one was connected by buried firing wire to a daisy-chain of Claymore mines camouflaged across the slope. The American Sergeant had thought long and hard about this moment. He had visualized a Russian infantry attack and imagined how they might attempt to overwhelm the fort.

He selected the two clackers labeled 'South' and released their small safety bails, then squeezed down on the triggers.

There was a split-second delay; a moment where the battlefield seemed to still and for an instant the big Sergeant fretted that the firing lines had been severed. He raised his head above the highest sandbag just as the first line of Claymore mines erupted along the southern flank of the Russian attack.

The mines had been cunningly laid in a staggered line to ensure the lethal blast from each device overlapped for maximum effect. All ten Claymores fired, two after a heartbeat of delay – and the devastation was appalling.

The jets of smoke and flame from each Claymore seem to leap from the ground as the earth heaved upwards and turned to fire and boiling smoke so thick that it blotted out the sun and cast the battlefield into temporary twilight. Men were hurled into the air and flung backwards by the layers of C-4 explosive each device contained. The explosions rumbled then cracked into a deafening thunder that rolled across the slope and echoed through the valley.

Inside each mine was a matrix of seven hundred steel balls set into an epoxy resin. When the ten Claymores detonated, thousands of fragments were flung across the sodden muddy ground. The Russians skirting the southern edge of the slope were slaughtered by the hammer blow of eruptions.

The Americans in the main trench stared with stunned awe at the terrible carnage. The air stank of blood and guts and vomit. Russian soldiers lay shattered in spreading muddy drifts of their own blood. Some infantrymen had been disemboweled by the flying steel, their guts hanging open as they sobbed and sagged and staggered. Many lay dead, their eyes sightless, their final expressions ones of tortured agony. Some men groaned and called desperately to comrades for help. One man sat in the grass, sobbing because he was blind. A Russian officer, his uniform shredded, his face and arms flensed by the flying steel balls, was so overcome by the horror that he sagged to his knees and wept inconsolably. Every man in his unit was dead or injured.

The living staggered across the slope in a daze, enveloped in the smoke and smothered by the stench of death. The Americans opened fire and their killing volley added to the savage slaughter.

Those Russians not affected by the massive chain of explosions cautiously veered across the slope, moving towards the northern edge of the rise as they continued to fight for ground. Sergeant Harley waited thirty seconds before he fired the daisy-chain of Claymores marked 'North'. He felt no remorse, no compassion as he squeezed the triggers tight in his fist. War was a brutal and savage business – and he was a veteran who had long ago come to terms with the demons of his conscience.

The northern flank of the slope erupted in a string of explosions. The ground heaved into the air in geysers of earth and stone and grass. The fireballs reached across the muddy slope and a second later the roiling smoke threw a merciful blanket over the gruesome carnage.

Ears ringing, their faces blackened with grit and grime, the beleaguered Americans lining the trench looked on in stunned astonishment. For long moments they had no targets to fire at, so thick was the smoke. They reloaded and gulped down water. When the acrid curtain of haze thinned and the battlefield was at last revealed, the slope was empty.

The Claymores had devastated the Russian troops and hammered the spirit from them. They fled to the valley's floor, their faces wide-eyed with terror so that only the dead and dying remained in the desolate wasteland.

One wounded Russian soldier left abandoned on the slope had both his legs severed. Another had been struck by the blast of a Claymore and hit in the groin by two bullets. He screamed for help, his face pulped bloody and beyond recognition. Everywhere the Americans looked there was a fresh scene of horror. Russians drowned in their own blood or lay quietly sobbing, their bodies shattered and the agony unbearable. One enemy soldier was on his knees in the mud, clutching at a stomach wound. Blood spilled through his fingers as he heaved and gasped for breath, his face twisted in excruciating agony. He swayed, then collapsed and never moved again.

*

The radio operator at Battalion HQ was red-faced and breathless as he snatched off his headphones and spun round in his chair. Lieutenant Colonel McCluskey stood hunched over the map-strewn table his brow furrowed and his expression thunderous.

"Message from Brigade, Colonel," the operator was a kid in his early twenties from California who had been deployed to the Battalion just a month earlier. "Reinforcements are on their way."

"What have we got coming, son?" McCluskey looked up from the map. He fetched a cigar from his top pocket and wedged it, unlit, into the corner of his mouth.

"A Company of eight AH-64 Apaches from the 159th Attack Reconnaissance Battalion are on their way from Warsaw, and the Brits are rushing 'The Devil's Children' squadron of Challenger 2 tanks forward. They're deploying out of Suwalki."

"The Devil's Children?"

"The Queen's Royal Hussars, sir. Fourteen MBTs."

"How long before the Brits arrive?" McCluskey worried the end of the cigar like a dog gnawing on a bone. His latest intelligence report had the Russian tank column driving south west on a road that skirted the lake. If they maintained their current route, the Russian armor would reach a critical strategic intersection near the little village of Wolownia where they could link up with an east-west road that was three kilometers behind the Allied line.

"Thirty minutes, sir."

McCluskey grunted. The Brit tankers had earned a reputation in the war as being tough bastards to beat in a fight. While not the most audacious or daring men to have ever driven armor, they were well lead and highly regarded throughout NATO for their dogged defense. The Lieutenant Colonel prayed the British tanks would reach the intersection before the Russians and then put the column of T-90s temporarily out of his mind. If the British responded quickly, the Challenger 2s would be able to hold up the enemy advance long enough for other NATO units to converge. Instead, he turned his attention back to the COP marked on his map with the notation, 'B 0-6'. The outpost was located on the northern shores of a lake. McCluskey leaned close to read, but the name of the waterway was written in Polish. It didn't matter. What mattered was that an isolated American Platoon defending the position were in the way of an entire Divisional attack that, according to his S2, no one in Allied lines had seen coming.

McCluskey turned and barked a question to the staff crammed into the tent. "Any word on Captain Gatfield?"

"He's dead, sir," someone on the far side of the headquarters tent spoke. A female lieutenant pushed through the crowd of milling bodies. She had a headset slung around her neck. "He was killed when the Russian artillery hit Becejty. No one from Company HQ survived the attack."

McCluskey grunted. He hadn't held a high opinion of Gatfield, but he felt obliged to give the news a moment of solemn silence. "What about this Captain Anson from Intelligence? Have we found him?"

"He's at Regimental HQ, sir."

McCluskey snatched the cigar from the corner of his mouth and his eyes glittered with relish. "Good. Get the son-of-a-bitch on the blower, pronto."

It took two long minutes for the line to connect. Colonel McCluskey spoke briefly and listened for a long time. He ended the conversation with the Intelligence Captain by asking a question.

"Would you confirm that at a court martial?"

When McClusky hung up the phone, he turned and hunted the room until his venomous gaze settled on the portly figure of Major Wayland Young.

Chapter 9:

Even before the smoke had cleared, the Russian mortars resumed their killing tempo, lobbing death onto the crest of the knoll to cover the retreat of the shattered infantry. The Americans were forced back down into their trenches as the explosions heaved and hurled the blood-soaked ground. One mortar round struck the lip of the main dugout, killing three Americans at the southeast corner and collapsing a length of the trench. Two more men were buried in the violent eruption. A Corporal screamed foully; his lower leg speared clean through by a blade-like shard torn from a shattered wooden post. Sergeant Harley and four others raced to the scene and dug the two buried men out of the earth with their bare hands. They emerged screaming, covered in muddy soil but otherwise unharmed. The dead were left where they fell.

Ponting kept an anxious eye on the smoke sifted slope, searching for signs of the next Russian attack. He flinched as fragments from a mortar round thudded close to a chink in the sandbag wall he had been peering through. Somewhere further along the trench a man screamed in shrill agony. The noise pierced the relentless din of the Russian bombardment and set his nerves on edge. He heard his breath come with a tremulous whimper. He covered the sound with a cough and when he peered back through the gap between the sandbags, he saw sudden movement on the valley floor. He stiffened instinctively.

Sergeant Harley came dashing along the length of the trench, his face working with agitation. The man seemed to be everywhere at once. "The Russians are preparing to attack again."

"I know," Ponting put his eye back to the crevice. The floor of the valley was obscured in drifting black smoke so that his view of the milling Russian Army was veiled and intermittent. But through the drifting skeins of haze, he could see at least a dozen BMP-2s forming up along the northern edge of the valley. Careless of the threat of anti-tank weapons, the armored troop carriers were preparing to advance up the face of the lower slope.

The rising ground had been turned into a muddy cratered quagmire by the relentless hammer of the enemy's artillery barrage, but the lower plateau of the knoll remained accessible to tracked vehicles. The final hundred meters of the gradient was too steeply inclined for armor to scale… but if the enemy was allowed to reach the lower escarpment, the fight would be over. From there, the infantry would have just a short sprint to reach the crest, with every step of their charge under the flailing menace of autocannons.

"We've got to hit them with the Javelins and the AT-4s before they can reach the high ground," Harley insisted.

Ponting hesitated. If he gave the order, he committed the last of his anti-tank weapons. Once they were expended, there would be nothing to prohibit the Russians from storming the lower plateau unhindered. He was assailed with indecision and doubts.

"Lieutenant!" Harley insisted. The first of the Russian vehicles were trundling towards the rise, throwing up a hail of mud from their steel tracks, their engines belching black gouts of diesel exhaust. Packed into the protective cargo bay of each vehicle would be seven or eight Russian infantrymen, armed and readying themselves to storm the crest.

Ponting forced himself to draw breath, then jerkily nodded his head. It was the last card he had left to play. "Pass the word to open fire."

Sergeant Harley cupped his hands to his mouth and shouted across the bomb-ravaged space between the main trench and the heavy weapons pit where the Javelin crews waited, his voice competing with the rising throaty roar of revving Russian engines. "Take out the lead BMPs!"

The closest Russian vehicles were less than three hundred meters from the barbed wire perimeter of the COP. From that range, the lethal Javelin missiles could not miss.

The first Russian troop carrier blew apart with a percussive roar like a thunderclap. The sound slammed against the sky and rumbled across the valley. The vehicle erupted in a ball of orange flame and flying metal fragments. A moment later the fire turned into a towering column of oily black smoke.

"Hit the bastards again!" Sergeant Harley's voice was savage with triumph.

The second BMP-2 seemed to flatten under the force of the devastating explosion as the Javelin missile struck. The steel sides of the troop carrier blew outwards and the vehicle's squat turret was ripped from the hull and sent catapulting across the sky, shooting sparks and smoke.

The enemy infantry in the troop carrier were killed in the shattering explosion. The trailing Russian vehicles opened fire on the crest of the ridge with their turret-mounted autocannons, continuing to advance up the muddy incline with dogged resolve.

A third BMP-2 was struck and destroyed by a Javelin missile before the Russians reached the lower plateau. The lead vehicle slewed about in a shower of mud to position itself within a shallow fold of ground. The rear doors slammed open and a handful of Russian soldiers burst from the steel belly of the vehicle and threw themselves down in the mud. A man carrying a light machine gun was hit in the throat by American fire. He screamed when he was struck and flailed his arms in the air. He fell into a shell crater, still thrashing, spraying blood. The rest of the disgorged infantry crawled to the lip of the crater and returned fire on the American position. The wounded man was left screaming a terrible wail of agony that made the frightened young soldiers nearby look anxiously around. The Russian officer leading the men crawled over to the wounded soldier and saw the bright blood gushing from between the man's fingers. His face was swollen and distorted, strangled for air. The officer unholstered his pistol, pressed the barrel against the dying man's temple, and fired once.

Four more BMP-2s reached the lower plateau and unloaded their cargoes of infantry. Under the furious flail of the vehicle's autocannons, slowly the Russian infantry began to advance.

"Fire the AT-4s!"

The four 84mm single-shot anti-tank weapons were a last resort. With a range of just a few hundred meters they were unguided and inaccurate compared to the lethal killing power of the Javelins. The Javelin crews fired the weapons, hitting two of the Russian troop carriers. Two of the missiles flew wide of their targets and disappeared into the blanket of smoke.

The Russian infantry were forced to claw for every inch of blood-soaked ground they gained. Some soldiers found small cover and fired on the ridge, rather than risk advancing into the waiting hail of death. Some men pushed forward bravely on their hands and knees, driven to heroic suicide by their officers. A man carrying a green flag was hit in the shoulder and spun around by the impact. He pirouetted in the mud and then fell. The flag was snatched up by a man following who carried it a full ten yards further up the slope before he was struck by half-a-dozen bullets and killed instantly.

Four more Russian BMP-2s reached the lower escarpment.

Guy Ponting sensed the inevitability of the enemy's assault. There were simply too many Russians with too much firepower for them to be resisted any longer. The slope of the knoll was littered with bodies heaped in rows like tidelines on a beach showing where the fight had ebbed and flowed, and the stench of death was a miasma that seemed to overpower even the acrid reek of cordite and smoke. Ponting joined the men at the parapet and fought as a rifleman because there was nothing else to be done. The men needed no orders, and the Javelin teams had exhausted their supply of missiles and fired the last of the AT-4s. There was nothing left to do but fight. He saw a Russian officer near the open doors of a BMP-2 and took aim. He was a young, pale-faced man with a flat hard face who was waving the Russian troops out of their APCs and marshalling them towards the ridge. He was shouting orders, grabbing men by the arms and shoving them into position. A stray bullet clanged off the steel hull of the vehicle he was standing next to. The officer ignored the danger with contemptuous disregard.

Ponting sighted on the man and pulled the trigger. The M4 juddered against his shoulder and roared. The bullets slammed into the Russian officer's head making it jerk. The shattering impact smashed a fist-sized chunk of bone and brain out of the Russian's skull. He collapsed to the ground, his heels kicking in nerveless spasms for a few seconds before he stilled.

For Ponting the whole battle became reduced to a small patch of mud and blood amidst a cauldron of smoke and noise. He seemed to lose all sense of time and any awareness of what was happening with fighting further along the trench. In the background the Russian mortars still fell like rain and the explosions still shook the ground beneath his feet, but all of his concentration was now on killing.

Two more Russian APCs reached the lower plateau and more Russian infantry spilled onto the slop and began the perilous ascent.

The Americans began running low on ammunition. Sergeant Harley went along the length of the trench collecting magazines from the dead and badly wounded. A Private at the northwest end of the trench was somehow hit in the thigh by a mortar fragment. He swore bitterly, clapped a hand over the wound to stem the flow of blood and fished around for a field dressing. He pulled down his pants, clenched his jaw and dressed the wound, then returned to the fire step and resumed shooting with his pants still bunched around his ankles.

A Russian soldier suddenly emerged from the smoke just thirty yards from the crest. He was staggering and dazed, his muddy uniform shredded. He was wearing a mask of blood through which his crazed eyes showed white. He had a green flag in his hand, using the wooden pole like a crutch. He had been shot in the leg and both arms. He stopped suddenly and swayed as though struck by a gust of wind. He cried out something in hoarse Russian and then collapsed to his knees. His head was thrown back, his face lifted to the smoke-smeared sky when Sergeant Harley shot the man in the chest and killed him.

"They're overwhelming us and we're running low on ammo," Harley said as the Russian carrying the flag was flung down into the mud.

"Claymores?"

"All that's left is the line in front of the wire."

"Fire them?"

"Not yet," the Sergeant said. "Not until the Russians make their final charge."

Ponting pulled the pin on a grenade and hurled it into the haze of no-man's land. The explosion flashed red amongst the swirling smoke. Somewhere a man grunted and then screamed in pain.

"There's no line of retreat," Ponting peered along the gloomy length of the trench and figured maybe fifteen men were dead or injured. There was no way the Platoon could fall back and leave those injured men to the care of the Russians. Nor was surrender an option. After the bloody toll the Americans had extracted, the Russians would be in a murderous mood. There would be no mercy.

Sergeant Harley seemed to read his young Lieutenant's dire thoughts. He smiled mirthlessly. His face was thick with grime and sweat and spattered blood, so that he looked like some evil apparition arisen from hell. "Then we'll just have to kill them all," he said.

Along the rise of the knoll a wall of Russian infantry suddenly burst into view, screaming as they charged through the smoke, firing from the hip as they ran. Sergeant Harley threw down his M4 and dived for the dangling clackers that would trigger the last Claymore mines.

The five remaining Claymores had been set in front of the perimeter wire, each mine staggered and positioned to ensure a solid killing zone that would sweep the slope of enemy. As Sergeant Harley squeezed the clacker that joined the daisy-chain of mines together, the crest of the knoll was rocked by a seismic tremor.

The Claymores exploded and the wall of the trench seemed to shift an inch. Sandbags were thrown down from the parapet and sections of earth began to give way. Down on the slope of the knoll the scene of devastation was apocalyptic. The mines had detonated at the same moment the Russian infantry had gathered themselves for the final assault on the crest. The combined blasts caught the charging enemy in a hail of screaming steel and cut them down like a scythe. In the aftermath of the ear-ringing explosions a new sound rose; it was the wailing shrieks of those Russians who were cruelly injured, thrown down, broken and flensed by the hail of death. Smoke roiled above the crest like a venting volcanic eruption that could be seen for miles.

Guy Ponting dared a peek above the lip of the trench and gaped in awe and horror. There were dozens of Russians dead and just as many crying out in bloody agony. One man was on fire, his uniform alight and smoldering as he flailed and shrieked in the mud. Another Russian knelt in the dirt, an arm missing. He bent over slowly and vomited blood.

The agonized screams of the dying faded and then came again, louder and strident, turning into an exultant roar of triumph; a high-pitched bellow of elation.

Ponting looked right and, incredibly, through the smoke saw his own looming defeat. He stared in helpless horror. A second Russian flanking attack was surging through the barbed wire perimeter at the southeast corner of the compound, and he realized with profound despair that the fighting and the dying had all been a vain folly.

It was over.

Fort Suicide was about to fall, and they were all going to die.

*

Under the cover of the main attack, with their movement concealed by the cacophony of smoke and mortar explosions, a Platoon of Russian veterans from the war in the Baltics had crept stealthily along the southern face of the slope.

The Platoon's task had been to approach the outpost and mount an assault once the Americans were engaged against the main attack force, cutting their way through the coiled perimeter wire and overwhelming the defenders.

Once in position, the outflanking force had waited until the Army's attack had reached a crescendo. The men were under the lip of the trench, hidden in a small fold of ground. They could see the coiled wire that marked the perimeter just twenty yards ahead of where they lay in the mud. The razor wire had been severed in three places by artillery and mortar fire. There was no need to cut a path through – the breach awaited only the right moment to attack.

The attackers listened to the rise and fall of the battle's noise, judging the advance by the sounds of gunfire. They had sensed the moment had arrived just a few seconds before the Americans fired their Claymore mines. They had risen to their knees and filled their lungs to make the charge when the ground beneath them suddenly heaved and the Russian attack along the battlefront had been cruelly decimated and driven back. Now the outflanking Platoon was alone on the ridge while the rest of the Army was in retreat. The Lieutenant commanding the assault cursed his luck, and then remembered that young Russian officers were expected to be the arbiters of their own fortune.

Distracted or not, the Americans would be exhausted and unsuspecting. The Lieutenant still had the element of surprise.

In the dreadful screaming that followed the Claymore mine explosions the young impulsive Lieutenant sprang suddenly to his feet, emerging like a ghostly apparition in the drifting tendrils of smoke.

"Obvinyat!" he cried, his shout just one more shrieking voice in the clamor and the chaos. "Charge!"

*

Guy Ponting saw the menacing grey shapes suddenly spring from the ground and come swarming up the slope and through the shell-ravaged wire. They were screaming like fiends, roaring a strangled battle-cry as they breached the outpost's perimeter and loomed over the lip of the trench. For a split-second the Lieutenant recoiled in shock and befuddled incomprehension. He felt the cold clammy dread of failure slide in his chest. Then, impulsively, he was seized by a warrior's red-mist of outrage. Anger swelled within him; a cold, savage fury he had never felt before. It seemed to slow time and elevated the small details of the moment into stark relief. He saw a Russian officer, a pistol in his hand and his uniform smeared in mud. The man's face was a brutal scarred snarl, his eyes black in the sallow unshaven face. He wore no helmet; his hair was brown, crusted with dirt.

Ponting filled his lungs and cried his own defiant, incoherent challenge, then went surging along the trench and into the snapping jaws of death.

"Kill the bastards!" Ponting's M4 had a fresh magazine loaded, and as he ran towards the threat, he fired from the hip, aiming up into the mass of grey shapes. He saw the Russian officer recoil, struck in the arm and chest by his ragged volley. He emptied the magazine and turned the weapon in his hand, wielding it as a club as he reached the collapsed end of the trench where the Russian shells had killed and buried a handful of his men. He saw a Russian soldier's weapon spit flame and heard the chattering roar of the gun firing. He felt hot wind flutter past his face and slap meatily into a sandbag beyond his shoulder, the passage of the bullets so close that he staggered.

"Kill the bastards! Drive them back down the slope!" he cried. The end of the trench was a ramp of loose caved-in earth, strewn with the bodies of the Americans who had died during the fighting. Ponting scrambled over the corpses on his hands and knees, drenched in mud and blood, and came to his feet in the midst of the Russian attackers.

"Fire! Cut them down!"

He emerged into the open and into a space of crater-strewn ground bordered by the tangled wire and the blackened twisted carcass of the burned-out Humvee. The Russians had the advantage. They had breached the COP's defenses and had achieved total surprise. Two of the enemy soldiers opened fire on the dark pit, spraying the trench's length with a chattering hail of bullets.

"Hit the bastards with everything we've got!"

Sergeant Harley and several other men had seen the Russians and heard their own young Lieutenant's berserker battle-cry. They followed Ponting up the slippery earthen ramp and into the fray.

The two sides were close enough to see the snarling savage faces of their enemies. Sergeant Harley shot a Russian infantryman in the head and felt the warm spatter of the man's blood as he dropped. Another enemy soldier sagged to his knees and retched. Behind him an American soldier cried out in sharp pain and the Sergeant turned to see a man with a knife buried in the side of his neck.

Guy Ponting slipped on the tangled mess of a Russian soldier's intestines and he went down onto one knee. A Russian saw the American officer stagger and lunged for the kill, wielding his empty AK-74 like a club. Ponting rolled to the side and heard the butt of the Russian weapon smack into the mud. He kicked out and hit the man hard in the knee with the heel of his boot. The enemy soldier grunted and staggered back a pace, his injured leg threatening to collapse beneath him. Ponting lashed out with his boot a second time and missed. The Russian swung his weapon again and Ponting rolled away from a blow that would have shattered his spine if it had connected. He scrambled to his feet, his M4 in his hand, and he thrust the barrel into the Russian's chest. The enemy soldier had no idea Ponting's weapon was empty. He threw up his hands and his face turned bloodless white, the savage madness in his eyes turning swiftly to naked fear. Ponting seized the small second of advantage. He lashed out with the weapon at the man's eyes, the cold steel barrel ripping flesh from the Russian's cheek, then quickly reversed the gun and clubbed the enemy soldier across the head. The Russian toppled backwards and Ponting went after him, his hands clawed and his teeth bared. He fell on the Russian's heaving chest and he was panting and snarling as his fingers locked around the flailing man's throat, his grip tightening remorselessly until the Russian gave a final strangled wheeze of foul breath and went limp beneath him.

Ponting came to his feet in a disoriented daze, but with the red-mist of madness still upon him. Three Americans were down, dead in the mud, but the Russians were edging backwards. He dared not let them regain the momentum.

"Kill the bastards!"

More Americans were springing from the trench to take the fight to the Russians. RTO Skinner shot two Russians with a burst of close-range automatic fire that caught both the enemy soldiers in the guts. One of the men clutched his hands to his stomach and folded forward with a pitiful groan of agony. The second Russian staggered backwards but incredibly stayed on his feet. He sprayed a short burst of fire into the air above Skinner's head then drew a knife from his belt and came forward with a roar, blood gushing from his wounds. Skinner reached for his sidearm, but before he could draw the M9 Beretta on his hip, Sergeant Harley turned, saw the danger, and shot the Russian in the face from point-blank range.

Ponting spun wild-eyed looking for the enemy. There were men all around him, swearing and grunting and snarling in savage life-and-death struggles. The Russians were being driven back from the trench's edge. A burst of automatic fire sounded hugely loud from behind him and a flicker of muzzle flash lit the smoke-filled cauldron in an instant of lurid orange. He saw RTO Skinner on his knees and another man dead on his back, his arms flung wide and a blood-rimmed hole in the middle of his forehead.

A Russian, his eyes wide with blood-lust, charged out of the smoke. He was a huge giant of a man with arms and legs like tree-trunks and a brutal, cruel face. He had an AK-74 on his hip. He fired from close range but the weapon clicked on an empty magazine. He reversed the weapon without losing step and clubbed an American to death with a single swinging blow, breaking the man's neck. Skinner fired and struck the Russian in the left leg. The enemy soldier staggered and took another faltering pace forward, the snarling rage still in his face. Sergeant Harley turned on his heel, saw the Russian, and kicked him hard in the groin. The huge man swayed like a tree in a storm. Harley kicked him again and the soldier toppled sideways to his knees. The Sergeant slit the Russian's throat with his bayonet.

The ground was awash with blood. One Russian lost his footing on the crumbling lip of the trench and fell into the pit where two Americans were waiting for him. He screamed once as he died. A Russian Sergeant became tangled in the coiled razor wire and lashed out like a wild animal in a snare until one of the Americans shot him twice; once in the chest and once in the groin.

Then, finally, the Russians were going backwards, hesitantly at first and then more quickly as they saw the body of their dead Lieutenant in the mud and realized they were without leadership. Ponting snatched for a fresh magazine and slammed it into his M4. He fired into the retreating Russians, but they were already just vague shapes in the smoke. He kept firing until the magazine was empty.

"That was a damned-near thing," Sergeant Harley rasped, his chest heaving like a bellows. He bent double and put his hands on his knees to suck in deep gulping breaths. "Christ!"

Ponting nodded, his face was spattered with blood and streaked with dirt. He gasped then glanced down the slope and saw the ground was empty of danger. The Russians had gone. "God Almighty, we were lucky!"

Weary men staggered dazedly in and out of the smoke, gathering up weapons and carrying the wounded back to the trench. Ponting stared at the appalling carnage of violence as though the entire fight had been a dreadful nightmare he was only now waking from. His hands began to shake and his breath came in short sharp sobs of shock as the red-mist of his rage dissolved.

Down in the valley the Russian mortars began firing again.

*

There was no mistaking the heavy thumping clatter on the air. Sergeant Harley turned and searched the sky, his eyes narrowing as he sought anxiously for the source of the sound. It faded then came again, louder and closer. Finally, Harley spotted the line of dark specks, hugging the horizon as they approached from the west. The big Sergeant gave a whoop of relief and triumph. One by one the beleaguered Americans lifted their heads to the clouds and a ragged, exhausted cheer rang around the outpost.

The eight AH-64 Apache helicopters from the 159th Attack Reconnaissance Battalion swarmed over the battlefield with the 30mm M230E1 chain guns in their chin turrets spitting flames and spewing death.

The hail of high explosive shells hit the first line of BMP-2s and then the Apaches swooped across the valley floor like a pack of wolves on the hunt. Bright flashes of light flared amongst the smoke-shrouded gloom. Two of the Russian armored troop carriers stationery on the lower plateau of the slope burst into flames and exploded, killing a handful of Russian soldiers who had ducked behind the vehicles to seek shelter from the gut-melting terror. The hail of cannon fire churned the earth and seemed to dissolve it into a boiling fog of dust and mud. The thunder of the clattering heavy machine guns was like the sound of a storm-surging river in flood.

The Apaches made their first pass over the valley floor, cutting a broad swathe through the Russian attack. Trees disappeared in the whirlwind of shredding fire, men were cruelly hacked down and minced to pulp. Three more BMP-2s in the valley exploded, killing several of the Russian mortarmen working slavishly to serve their weapons. The ground was left furrowed and churned. The thunder of deafening noise abated as the Apaches swept east and the shrill whine of their passage faded for a moment. Then the attack helicopters hung in their air and turned back towards the knoll. Each of the eight Apaches was armed with eight Hellfire missiles and thirty-eight 70mm Hydra rockets. The onboard AN/APG-78 Longbow radars prioritized targets, and the pilots began their bloody work.

It was a slaughter to end a morning of brutal killing as the AH-64s unleashed their payload of missiles and rockets. The weapons launched on fiery plumes of white smoke that streaked across the sky and burst upon the nearest Russian troop carriers. In just sixty lethal seconds forty-two BMP-2s were destroyed and hundreds of Russian infantry, killed, maimed or injured. The valley floor was strewn with carnage; towering black columns of oily smoke, burned out mangled metal carcasses, and dead bodies lying in spattered puddles of gore and blood. And long after the Apaches had expended their munitions and disappeared back beyond the western horizon, still the Russian vehicles in the valley burned and the wounded across the battlefield groaned and moaned and slowly bled to death.

Thirteen kilometers north of Suwalki, and several kilometers behind Allied lines, the fourteen British Challenger 2 tanks from 'The Devil's Children' squadron of the Queen's Royal Hussars were hull down north of Wolownia when the flying column of Russian T-90s suddenly burst into sight.

Using the lake to protect their right edge, the British tanks were arrayed forward of a vital intersection. The Russian tanks approached at high speed, eager to secure the critical crossing and thus endanger the entire flank of the Allied defense. They trundled down the road trailing a huge column of spreading dust in their wake, throwing caution to the wind in exchange for a lightning strike that would collapse NATO's resistance all along the Polish border. The British tanks waited until the closest enemy MBTs were within a thousand meters and then opened fire.

The head of the Russian column was savagely mauled. The first eight T-90s were destroyed in the opening seconds of the brutal firefight. Four of the MBTs exploded into fireballs of smoke and flame. Four more vehicles were disabled by strikes to their running gear, rendering them immobile.

The British tank crews were trained to a razor's edge of ruthless efficiency. The Russian tanks were too close to make use of their long range Reflekt ATGM's and too far from the British to rely on their own tank's armor-piercing rounds to ensure a kill.

The positional disadvantage caused chaos within the Russian ranks. Needing desperately to close on the enemy, the Russian commander ordered his armored column forward under cover of smoke. The British MBTs fired a second time and then withdrew to the outskirts of the village, popping their own smoke as they fell back, leaving six more T-90s destroyed or disabled in their wake. Manfully the rest of the T-90s surged forward.

One Challenger 2 was caught broadside reversing to its secondary position and was fired upon by a T-90 as the tank burst through the white swirling veil of haze. At six hundred yards, not even the British tank's Dorchester armor could protect the vehicle. The Russian AP round tore straight through the Challenger's hull, immobilizing the engine. A follow-up shot just eight seconds later destroyed the British tank completely, blowing the seventy-ton beast into a million jagged metal fragments as it exploded, killing the crew inside. Another Challenger 2 took a hit on its right-side roadwheels, leaving it stranded. The four-man crew bailed out of the stricken tank and scampered to safety uninjured.

From the cover of the village, the remaining British Challenger 2s fired a third time, scoring more hits. The rolling grass fields west of the lake's edge were now littered with burning debris and churned muddy by tank tracks. More than half of the Russian armored attack force had been destroyed or disabled in just ten furious minutes of frantic turmoil.

Smoke columns towered into the sky, so thick that they blotted out the sun and plunged the battlefield into eerie half-light.

Unsupported by motorized infantry that could have closed the range on the British Challengers and flushed them from their hull-down positions around the village, the Russian commander reluctantly signaled for his surviving tanks to withdraw. They fled the field behind more smoke canisters, withdrawing all the way to the war-torn border.

A few miles further east, at the Lithuanian farmhouse that served as the Russian command post, the three-star Colonel general of tanks listened to the reports coming in from the battlefield with rising agitation and finally unholy rage.

His tanks had withdrawn, surrendering the captured village of Becejty and failing to secure the vital crossroads at Wolownia. In the Szelment valley, the situation was even worse; the American outpost remained stubbornly defiant and almost fifty BMP-2s and several hundred infantry had died in the attempt to win the high ground.

Elsewhere along the battlefront the news was little better. North of the valley, Russian motorized infantry supported by T-72s had broken the Allied line in two separate locations, routing a German *Bundeswehr* Company. But in both instances NATO troops had been able to shore up the breach in their lines before the Russians had been able to kick the door wide open and storm into the enemy's rear.

Now, the advantage of surprise had been lost and not an inch of ground gained.

"This should have been ruthless! Efficient!" the Colonel general punched the map table with his fist to punctuate each word, then turned a malevolent eye around the farmhouse, looking for someone to blame – something to vent his anger upon. The functionary officers who were gathered around the edges of the room cringed, aware of their commander's blazing temper. In a fit of impotent frustration, the Colonel general swept the maps from the table and hammered his fist down again.

"Fuck the Americans! Fuck their NATO allies!"

For a long moment the room crackled with tension, then the Colonel general stirred himself and set about bringing order to the chaos. The greatest part of his Army was still uncommitted. He had entire Divisions of armor and mechanized infantry waiting on the border.

He would release them all, and in the process, he would drown every Allied soldier who dared defy him in a river of blood. The Americans and their Allies had repelled the first thrust, but now he would show his enemies exactly how a Russian warrior fought.

He sought out a radio operator and stabbed the man in the chest with his finger. "Get our field commanders on the line immediately. Tell them to prepare for another attack. We're going back to war, and this time we're going to do it the old-fashioned way."

It was time to unleash hell.

Chapter 10:

The Black Hawk was unmarked and painted black, rather than the typical military green. It came from out of the west, flying nap-of-the-earth, while in the sky overhead two USAF F-16 Vipers turned lazy circles in the clouds, white contrails in their wake.

The Black Hawk hugged the contours of a small ridge then swept across the surface of the lake, stirring the water as it passed. It leaped up at the last minute and appeared over the COP's landing zone, its downdraft kicking up clouds of swirling dust. The pilot sideslipped the helicopter to avoid the bomb-cratered edge and flared out for a landing.

The helicopter settled smoothly and the Black Hawk's thumping rotors began to slow as the twin turbine engines spooled down. The cargo door slid open and General Chris Buford stepped down to the shell-ravaged ground.

Buford was SACEUR, (Supreme Allied Commander Europe) a United States Air Force Four-star General and a distant relative of John Buford Jr. who had gained fame as the commander of the 1st Division of the Union's Cavalry Corps at the Battle of Gettysburg.

He was a tall, lean man with piercing dark eyes and a hawk-like nose. The hair beneath his cap was black, peppered with streaks of grey. He was dressed in simple camouflage combat fatigues. He propped his hands on his hips and cast a searching gaze across the skyline, missing nothing. The air reeked of smoke and blood and death.

Behind the General a handful of staff officers disembarked the Black Hawk. The last man out of the helicopter was Lieutenant Colonel Chuck McCluskey, commander of the American infantry Battalion.

Exiting the Black Hawk into the artillery-torn smoke-obscured slaughterhouse of the knoll was like stepping into a different world. The air was thick and heated, the ground soaked in blood and littered with smoldering debris. The forward-facing slope was strewn with mangled Russian bodies and gore.

Guy Ponting approached the helicopter drenched in blood. His face was grime-stained and his uniform dark with mud. General Buford seemed to shudder in reaction to the stench of sweat and cordite and corruption that wafted across the battlefield. He stared at the young Lieutenant, appalled. Behind Ponting the rest of the surviving Platoon members emerged from their trenches like ghosts from a gruesome nightmare.

Past Ponting's shoulder the eastern skyline appeared smudged with smoke, and in the foreground the slope down to the valley's floor was a churned and burned charnel house strewn with death.

"Lieutenant Ponting?" Buford held out his hand, still numbed and awed by the carnage. "I'm Chris Buford. I'm sorry for the unannounced visit, but I wanted to shake the hands of the band of heroes who held up the entire Russian offensive… and I wanted also to extend a personal apology. It seems that a breakdown in our intelligence network resulted in you and your men being abandoned," SACEUR gave Lieutenant Colonel McCluskey a significant sideways glance. McCluskey had briefed SACEUR on Major Wayland Young's decision to bury Ponting's report of an imminent Russian attack during the flight to the battlefront. "You can rest assured that kind of error will never happen again. The man responsible will be court-martialed."

Ponting shook SACEUR's hand, still in a daze. His ears were ringing, his body twitching and trembling with the after-effects of the fear and the horror. "We have wounded, sir…" he said.

"Medivac birds are inbound as we speak," Lieutenant Colonel McCluskey intercepted. "You and all your men will be flown back to Warsaw, Lieutenant. You've done everything and more your duty demanded of you. Reinforcements will relieve your men. Our latest ELINT suggests the Russians are preparing for another attack," SACEUR went on to explain. "In a couple of hours from now this valley is going to be filled with Russian armor and infantry trying to push through our lines. You and your men have earned my respect and gratitude. Now it's time for a well-earned rest."

Ponting turned and searched the smoke-smudged horizon for a long contemplative moment, then turned back. He had stared down his fear and emerged from the fiery cauldron of battle somehow a changed man. "With respect, sir," he spoke through dry cracked lips. "We were here at the start of the fight and we'd like to be here to see it through to the end."

SACEUR smiled grim admiration. "Permission granted," he said then drew a deep breath and narrowed his eyes, surveying the terrain that would soon become one of the war in Europe's bloodiest battlefields. "Now, let's go and teach those Russian bastards a lesson they won't soon forget."

*

Throughout the rest of the long morning, Allied reserve forces streamed east through the bottleneck of Suwalki and began assembling on the far rim of the valley floor. Szelment had been abandoned by the Russians when they had withdrawn to the border. Now it was being turned into an Allied stronghold by a Battalion of German infantry. The approaching roads to the village had been blocked with rubble, the verges hastily mined. C-wire ringed the village outskirts, and in the houses that faced the Russians, narrow firing slits had been gouged out of the walls by engineers who worked with the urgency of men who knew their lives depended on it. Two stone farmhouses beyond the village were manned by German anti-tank crews and the forest a mile to the northwest was now occupied by an American Stryker Squadron supported by four A1 IM-SHORADs armed with Hellfire and Stinger missiles for air defense.

West of Fort Suicide the surviving British Challenger 2 tanks from 'The Devil's Children' squadron of the Queen's Royal Hussars had moved to the ruins of Becejty to act as a bulwark against the expected Russian advance, and as a ready-reserve that could be rushed forward to the front at a moment's notice.

And still more Allied reserves raced east towards the battlefront. British and American infantry were flown forward by a fleet of transport helicopters from Warsaw while Apache gunships and A-10 Warthogs prowled the sky overhead.

The American 16th Infantry Regiment's 1st Combined Arms Battalion were racing north from Augustow along choked roads, moving at a snail's pace. The presence of their two companies of Abrams MBTs on the battlefield might mean the difference between survival and abject defeat.

SACEUR coordinated the troop movements from the elevated rise of the knoll while Ponting watched the far horizon with binoculars. Three of his Platoon's survivors suffering minor wounds had been air-lifted back to Warsaw with the men who were too severely injured to continue the fight, but the rest of the unit had stoically remained. They slept, exhausted, in the shade of the trench and under the cover of makeshift tents while around them the ruins of the COP were transformed to a forward command post for the flank of the Allied Army.

Finally, just after 1pm, the Russian artillery barrage began anew, concentrating on the village of Szelment. The first incoming rounds destroyed a knot of buildings close to the main intersection. Houses burned and walls were collapsed under a tower of rising black smoke. The day was becoming warmer. The smoke from the morning had drifted away on the breeze revealing patches of blue sky and high cloud. To the south, from where the 16th Regiment's Combined Arms Battalion were anticipated, the sun shone down on empty roads and desolate farm fields.

"If the Russians come at us in force, we won't be able to hold them. Not with what we have assembled," Sergeant Harley gave his opinion.

Lieutenant Ponting kept the binoculars pressed to his eyes. A cloud front seemed to be building along the eastern horizon.

He stared at it carefully and felt a rising sense of ominous foreboding.

"We need those Abrams tanks," the Lieutenant swung the glasses to the south and stared at the empty terrain that was basking under bright shafts of afternoon sunlight. The pastures were a lush patchwork of rolling green hills, sprinkled with small fields of land ploughed brown and ready for planting. Ponting could see no distant dust cloud, no hint that somewhere over the horizon some thirty Abrams tanks and a host of Bradley Fighting Vehicles were imminent. "I just hope they get here in time."

*

The Russian artillery suddenly ceased fire and in the aftermath of their hellish hammering the world seemed eerily quiet with foreboding. Smoke hung in a dirty black pall over the village of Szelment and the forest to the northwest where the American Strykers lurked was ablaze.

Then the wind shredded the veil of smoke to reveal a phalanx of Russian armor emerging from the east and trundling down the slope into the valley. The Russian tanks advanced in long lines with an armored column of BMP-2s on each flank, leaving the earth churned and the tall grass flattened in their wake. The formation seemed to be given its rhythm by the cough of smoke canisters being fired from the lead T-90s as they reached the valley floor. Behind them, and just appearing on the skyline was a second phalanx of Russian T-72s supported by more troop carriers. Overhead three Su-25 ground attack jets appeared from within the low-lying skeins of smoke, their engines roaring as they came snarling low over the battlefield. The 'Frogfoots' unleashed a flurry of missiles into the forest where the American Strykers waited in ambush. Four M1126 combat vehicles were destroyed in the lethal fusillade. The American A1 IM-SHORADs returned fire on the Russian Su-25s, shooting one of the jets from the sky as they flashed low overhead. The stricken 'Frogfoot' had its right wing wrenched from the fuselage. In a shower of sparks and smoke it tumbled across the clouds and landed in a patch of farm field, exploding on impact.

The remaining Su-25s darted on towards the British Challenger 2 tanks around the bomb-ruined outskirts of Becejty. They flew past Fort Suicide, a mile to the north, skimming the contours of the ground as they thundered by. A shoulder-fired Stinger missile dashed after the Russian jets on a trail of white smoke but lost contact and exploded harmlessly. The Su-25s unleashed Vikhr laser-guided tube-launched missiles at four Challengers on the western edge of Becejty. Two Challengers were destroyed in the lightning attack before a pair of Polish F-16 Vipers flying a combat air patrol plunged from the high clouds and destroyed both 'Frogfoots'.

The action lasted less than two minutes. In the wake of the attack, several Strykers were destroyed, two British Challenger 2 MBTs blown apart, and all three Russian 'Frogfoots' shot down in flaring fireballs of flame and smoke.

And still the Russian phalanx of armor came on, the revving roar of their engines a sinister, menacing sound. The line of T-90s reached the eastern edge of Szelment and fighting broke out, the action concealed behind a great shroud of boiling smoke. Ponting saw flashes of flaming red light puncture the grey haze and then German infantry began streaming back across the valley. The T-90s surged through the village and out the western side, into open fields and into sight of two American infantry companies that were concealed behind hedgerows on the southern slope of the valley.

The Americans were armed with Javelin anti-tank weapons. One of the operators hunched over his weapon's CLU and stared at the image on his monitor. The closest T-90 was broadside to his position and less than a mile away. The operator adjusted the diopter ring on the eyepiece assembly to bring the Russian tanks into clear focus. Through the eyepiece he saw the weapon's status indicators all glowing green. He activated the weapon's seeker, and flashing track gates appeared in the CLU display. The gates were a visual indicator that the seeker was active. The operator adjusted the crosshairs to designate the center of the T-90's mass, locking the missile in the tube onto its target. The fingers of his right hand found the Attack Select switch on the handgrip. By default, the weapon was already set to 'top attack' mode.

Triggering the seeker had enabled the fire trigger. The operator took a long deep breath and began to breath out as he squeezed...

The Javelin missile leaped from the CLU, seemed to hang in the air for a moment, and then began to climb in to the sky. Six seconds later it plunged back to earth and tore through the top armor of the Russian tank, destroying it in a mighty thunderclap of fire and smoke. The rest of the Javelin teams along the hedgerow opened fire. Their job was to harass the flank of the armored attack. Men ducked and darted to reload while down in the valley the southern column of BMP-2s turned to brush the American troops aside. The Russian infantry in the cargo holds of the troop carriers exploded from the rear doors of their vehicles and waded into the long grass, weapons drawn and firing from the hip at the hedgerow. The Russian BMP-2 commanders turned their 30mm autocannons onto the low rise, shredding the foliage and stripping the Americans of shelter. The two infantry companies were forced to duck for cover by the fury of the Russian attack. Enemy soldiers buzzed in swarms. An American Lieutenant was shot in both legs and went down in the mud screaming. Another infantryman beside him was struck in the back of the head as he turned to shout for more ammunition. He died instantly.

"Fall back! Fall back!" an officer shouted and waved his arm, urging his men to abandon their primary positions for the safety of supplementary firing locations that NATO engineers had dug seventy meters higher up the gentle slope. The Russians reached the abandoned hedgerow and fired up the grassy rise. Twenty American infantrymen went down in the furious fusillade, caught in the open as they withdrew. Blood soaked the grass and more men died in gruesome agony.

"Fall back!"

The Americans had done their job; they had snapped at the heels of the Russian armored advance and as a consequence more than a dozen T-90s across the valley were smoldering ruins beneath black oily clouds.

An American infantryman turned and fired at the pursuing Russians, spraying the blood-slicked slope with a full magazine of chattering death from his M4. Three enemy soldiers were felled before the defiant American was finally cut down in a murderous crossfire and killed. More men lobbed grenades from the crest of the slope and a ragged chorus of coughing explosions echoed across the valley. Slowly, bitterly, the Americans retreated all the way to the top of the rise. The Russian infantry mounted an attack, reinforced by a handful of BMP-2s. Without armored support, and with precious few Javelin missiles remaining, the Americans were driven further south in disarray. Finally, the Russian officers recalled their men and the push across the valley's floor continued. The following tanks swerved past those that had been destroyed and continued to rumble forward. This was the Russian way of war; a massive steel fist that relied on sheer weight and brute force to bludgeon its way to victory. In the enemy's wake, over a hundred US soldiers lay dead or wounded.

SACEUR watched the shattered American infantry stream south in grim silence. He had miscalculated the Russian response. He had anticipated the enemy would sweep by the skirmishing flank attack and continue on, unchecked, towards the rise. But the Russians had turned on the American infantry columns with a fierce savagery that had stunned him. He bit his lip and frowned, then, as though it were an involuntary reflex, he turned and peered south with binoculars pressed to his eyes.

His expression was forlorn and troubled.

The 16th Infantry Regiment's 1st Combined Arms Battalion was still nowhere in sight.

*

The northern column of Russian BMP-2s, advancing on the far flank of the valley, brushed against the edge of the forest where the American Stryker Squadron was concealed. Hull-down MGSs pounded the Russian troop carriers to scrap metal as they passed. Then Apache AH-64 helicopters appeared on the horizon like a swarm of snarling hornets.

The Apaches came sweeping down the valley from the west, firing Hellfire air-to-surface missiles into the head of the Russian column, blunting its progress and turning the northern rim of the valley into a crucible of smoke and fire. The Hellfire missiles slammed into the BMP-2s, crumpling the front rank of troop carriers and causing chaos for those vehicles in the trail. Russian infantry spilled from their vehicles armed with 9K333 Verba MANPADS (man-portable air-defense systems). One of the operators climbed onto the hull of a BMP-2 and fired standing upright. The Verba's 9M336 surface-to-air missile leaped from the shoulder-fired tube and hung in the air for an instant, then went streaking across the sky in a looping arch trailing a thick tail of grey smoke. The missile locked on to an Apache that was turning sharply in the air and blew it from the sky. Another Russian operator dropped to one knee and fired at an Apache as it swooped overhead, the helicopter's 30mm M230E1 chain gun spitting venom as it passed in a thunder of terrifying clattering noise. The pilot of the Apache had no time to react. The Verba's missile sliced the tail rotor off the Apache and the chopper went spiraling crazily down the sky, exploding in a monstrous fireball of flames when it crashed to the ground. Three more Apache helicopters were shot down in a fierce minute of firefighting before the attack helicopters were forced to retreat west. Two A-10 Warthogs unleashed their deadly payloads into the phalanx of Russian armor before being chased off by more MANPADS fire.

The battlefield was a hellish nightmare of explosions and smoke and fire. But the Allied attacks on the flanking columns had served their purpose. The American infantry on the southern rim of the basin and the Strykers in the forest to the north of Szelment had suffered appalling losses, but in the process, they had forced the Russian advance to contract towards the center of the valley, sheering away from the dual threats to avoid the Americans gnawing at their edges.

The noise throughout the valley intensified. Russian tanks and APCs were strewn across the muddy ground. The smoke was so thick that several Russian vehicles collided on their relentless drive towards the knoll of high ground and the village of Becejty beyond it.

The American Cavalry Strykers emerged from the woods and charged bravely into the milling chaos, hunting through the smoke like a wild pack of wolves. In the first few minutes the Cavalry MGSs destroyed a handful of Russian BMP-2s before the American's ran across the guns of the Russian tanks.

The Strykers were no match for the heavily armored T-90s and the glorious charge quickly became a slaughter.

The American and Russian infantry fought their own personal war amongst the wreckage and ruins of the valley. The Cavalry troopers went forward into the smoke and caught the enemy in milling confusion. Dozens of Russians lay dead on the ground, killed when their APCs had been destroyed. Dozens more were numbed and dazed and disorientated, staggering and blood-spattered. A Russian Captain saw the Cavalry troopers through the swirling smoke and barked an urgent order to his men. A handful of nearby infantrymen responded but they were cut to pieces by a fusillade of automatic fire. The Americans overwhelmed the enemy troops and then the Javelin teams savaged the advancing lines of enemy tanks with more shoulder-mounted missiles. In quick succession, four more T-90s erupted in fireballs of smoke and flames, struck by Javelins from such close range that the weapons were unleashed in 'direct attack' mode; the missiles streaking straight for their targets rather than the default 'curve ball' attack.

Standing on the knoll and enveloped in drifting clouds of smoke, SACEUR peered into the haze and judged the battle's progress by the sound of the advancing Russian tanks and the pinpricks of fiery red explosions that punctuated the grey clouds of swirling smoke. In the deafening echo of the explosions, SACEUR heard the relentless chatter of automatic fire that told him the American Cavalry troopers were still in the fight. The Russian T-90s continued to bludgeon their way forward, still closing on the knoll despite being savaged by Javelin and Hellfire missiles. The air quivered with the constant percussion of explosions.

SACEUR sensed the closest Russian BMP-2s were approaching the foot of the slope. The Allied troops on either flank had done all they could to slow and savage the enemy's advance, but now there was nothing standing in the Russians way of victory other than his command post staff and a shrunken Platoon of soldiers who had already fought themselves to exhaustion.

He cast a glance sideways and saw Lieutenant Ponting and Sergeant Harley standing by the tangled perimeter wire, both men with binoculars to their eyes, both peering intently into the roiling smoke.

"We haven't done enough to dissuade the enemy," SACEUR sounded macabrely calm and detached. Guy Ponting lowered his binoculars and then flinched involuntarily as a stray flurry of enemy autocannon fire stitched the ground by his feet.

"They're stubborn, sir." There was nothing more to say.

SACEUR looked south. The 16th Infantry Regiment's 1st Combined Arms Battalion still had not arrived.

The General sighed and his shoulders slumped, then he turned to one of his aides standing attentively off to one side. "Call in the Black Hawks. We need to prepare to evacuate. Then radio the British. Tell the Challenger 2s to advance from Becejty and join the battle immediately."

*

"Somehow this don't seem right, y'know?" Sergeant Harley shouted above the chaos of the battlefield; the explosions, the whip-crack of automatic fire and the screams of the men who fought and died in the valley. He turned and stared around the perimeter of the outpost like it was hallowed ground, and then lifted his eyes to the sky where a small fleet of Black Hawk helicopters circled in the distance. "If we evacuate now, the god-damned Russians win," he growled. "We lost good men today. They died defending this place. Now we're going to retreat and give it up to the fucking enemy?"

The first of the Black Hawks came drifting down through the smoke and settled on the LZ. The cargo door opened and a handful of military aides hauled communications equipment and a collapsed field tent to the waiting chopper. The downdraft of the rotors cut through the veil of smoke so that for a moment, in the distance, the Sergeant and Lieutenant could see the column of British Challenger 2 tanks advancing. They were west of the knoll, following the road that ran along the northern lip of the valley. The Challengers were moving forward in a column, but as they rounded the knoll and came fully into view of the valley, they moved into a disciplined echelon formation. Lieutenant Ponting pointed.

"At least we get to live another day, and so do the rest of the Platoon. Those poor bastards are on a suicide mission."

The command staff evacuating the COP stopped loading the Black Hawks and turned to watch the British tanks with awe and macabre trepidation. There was less than a dozen of the Challengers, charging to certain destruction against more than fifty Russian T-90s and T-72s. The British opened fire in a blaze of heroic defiance and the battle quickly became a maelstrom of explosions and confusion, like a mesmerising dance to the death.

The fight across the valley's floor dissolved into clouds of dust and smoke. The Challenger 2s came off the road and swooped down the gentle rise onto the valley floor, firing on the move as they tried to close the range with the Russian tanks, attacking their exposed flank. The second line of Russian MBTs veered to meet the threat. Three T-72s exploded into black pyres of smoke before the first British tank had its roadwheels disabled by a close-range direct hit from a T-90. A second Challenger was encircled by a T-90 that scored a direct hit on the British tank's vulnerable rear armor. The Challenger seemed to shudder as the Russian sabot round plunged into the heart of the British tank. A split-second later it exploded in a hail of flaming fragments.

"The poor bastards…" Ponting muttered.

It was stirring and tragic; a scene from a mythical fable of heroism. The British tank crews fought the Russians to a temporary standstill until they were overwhelmed by the sheer weight of the Russian force. Four more Challenger 2 tanks were destroyed at close range and three more disabled. But the valiant British had cut a swathe of destruction through the Russian advance, destroying eight T-72s and three T-90s.

After the last British tank had been destroyed, a solemn forlorn pall descended over the battlefield. The Russians were in disarray, their solid line of MBTs shredded by the chaos of the savage dogfight. They moved quickly to realign themselves, the file closing up to fill the gaps that had been torn from their ranks.

And then, in the distance, a new thunder of gunfire echoed across the smoke-drenched sky.

*

The lead Abrams tanks of the 16th Infantry Regiment's 1st Combined Arms Battalion appeared across the rim of the southern slope, their main guns firing as they appeared as ghostly grey beasts against the skyline.

SACEUR saw the sudden flashes of flame leap from the muzzles of the advancing tanks through the roiling smoke and breathed a deep sigh of relief. He wheeled on his heel and seized an aide's arm. "We're not evacuating. We're not evacuating. We stand our ground. Get rid of the Black Hawks and order the 16th's rifle companies to swing through Becejty. I want them here!" he stamped his foot on the ravaged blood-soaked ground. "Right here!"

The Abrams spurred forward. There were almost thirty of the American tanks, dusty and mud-spattered, and low on fuel. Their opening salvo from the high ground tore into the flank of the Russian attack, hitting the T-90s in the front row broadside, destroying six enemy MBTs and disabling two more. And then they charged.

The lead Abrams surged down the same grassy slope where earlier the two Companies of American infantry had been routed. The commanders of the Russian tanks driving across the valley floor reacted with shock and began to turn their vehicles to meet the new threat head on. Steel tracks bit deep into the soft muddy ground as the T-90s slewed and their turrets turned.

"Make the bastards pay!" Guy Ponting snarled from the ruins of Fort Suicide. "Tear the fucking heart out of them!"

There was a narrow drainage ditch at the bottom of the slope. The Abrams jounced over the obstacle and for an agonizing moment the smoke billowed so thickly that from the crest of the knoll, the entire valley floor was obscured. Red violent flashes of light bloomed in the haze and the howling whine of revving engines sounded like the dying screams of ancient monsters. Then the sound came, carried clearly on the gentle breeze; the thunderous boom of the tanks firing, exchanging heavy punches at close range through the twitching smoke and a maelstrom of clamor.

Finally the smoke cleared and Ponting peered across the bowl of the valley, trying to make sense of the rising battle. He saw an Abrams fire at a T-90 through a swirling dust cloud. The Russian vehicle's turret was torn clean off the tank in an explosion of sparks and a great gout of oily smoke. Another T-90 was struck at close range from behind and blew apart in a hail of twisted steel. Then an Abrams ground to a halt streaming thick smoke from its hull. The hatches of the tank sprung open and through his binoculars Ponting saw four small figures running in dazed confusion. They dashed for their lives, weaving a ragged path through the twisting, turning tanks, trying to reach the rise of the knoll. Chattering machine gun fire stitched the ground at their feet. One of the crewmen suddenly stiffened and his back arched. He threw his hands in the air and then his knees sagged and he fell face-first into the mud.

The tank battle became a fight neither side had prepared for; a close-quarters gladiatorial battle in a colosseum of mud and blood. US doctrine of seeing the enemy first and getting the first shot to ensure victory didn't apply in a knife fight. At such perilously close range every mistake was fatal and survival depended on speed, agility and the quick reflexes of well-trained crews. Gradually the Americans gained the upper hand. Their crews were seasoned veterans of the war, having fought since the outbreak of hostilities across western Europe. The Russian three-man crews were new to fighting and now they were paying for their inexperience. In quick succession four T-90s and a handful of T-72s were destroyed; turned to twisted coffins of blackened smouldering metal by a succession of Abrams heavy punching sabot rounds. Smoke boiled, dust swirled and flashes of blinding fiery blooms lit the cauldron. Heavy machine gun fire chattered, adding its own menacing voice to the mayhem. An Abrams was struck on the turret from a front-on shot. The sabot round whanged away into the distance. The American commander inside his tank cringed as the thunderous sound of the deflection rang like a giant bell. He fired a snap-shot that destroyed the enemy T-90's track and left the Russian tank stranded in a boiling cloud of smoke.

Gradually, without any orders being given, the Russian tanks began to withdraw, choking the battlefield with white haze from their turret-mounted smoke launchers. The Abrams pursued the enemy like a pack of savage dogs, snapping at the heels of the Russian formation as it gradually edged back across the ravaged valley.

On the edges of the great tank battle, the Russian infantry still pushed forward. No longer contained inside the steel hulls of their troop carriers, the soldiers streamed towards the rise as if overcome with some suicidal madness. Spurred by their shouting officers the enemy troops came forward towards the knoll instead of falling back. The Russians were screaming as they ran, the sound drowned out by the hammering explosions of the tank battle. As they advanced, they fired up the slope into the grey haze.

The American Bradley Fighting Vehicles transporting the rifle companies of the CAB reached the ruins of Becejty and followed the road that wound along the edge of the lake. Unwilling to expose their troop carriers to the threat of Russian tank fire, the Company commanders parked behind the knoll and the two Companies of infantry spilled from their vehicles, tense and on edge. One entire Company ran up the dirt trail towards Fort Suicide. The second Company skirted the foot of the rise… and ran straight into the charging Russian infantry, catching the enemy on their flank as the Russians began to scale the lower incline.

The slope of the knoll erupted in a fierce blazing exchange of automatic gunfire. Ponting, SACEUR and Sergeant Harley threw themselves down into the trench as a wild burst of fire flailed across the outpost and the noise of the battle reached a new and dreadful crescendo. One of SACEUR's aides went down, shot in the face by a stray Russian bullet. The man was punched back by the impact, as if he had been struck by an invisible fist. The bullet caught the aide in the open mouth and exited through the back of his skull. His body twitched in the mud as the flies began to swarm gleefully around the sludge of his spattered brains.

The American infantry Company on the dirt road leading to the COP reached the crest of the knoll and swarmed past the trench, roaring a blood-curdling scream as they charged through the shredded remains of the barbed wire barrier. The Russians were caught between an attack to their front and an attack on their flank as the Americans swarmed down the slope to engage at close range. A Russian officer saw the threat and tried to turn some of his men to confront the new danger. A flurry of bullets caught him in the chest as he filled his lungs to scream the order. He was flung down into the muddy ground, dead. An American Sergeant was shot in the arm but ran on and kept firing, a Russian soldier threw himself down on the ground and feigned death. Two Russians snatched grenades off their webbing belts and lobbed them up the slope, killing three Americans and maiming four others who were cut down by fragments and left writhing in muddy agony. Then the two Companies of Americans halted their charges and fired into the Russians from point-blank range; concentrated withering bursts of gunfire that savaged the enemy advance and drove it back upon itself. The closest Russian soldiers recoiled in shock or looked for scant cover. Those following behind were cut down or began to edge fearfully backwards. The storm of shooting broke into a series of desperate, brutal spot fires of fury that erupted in a splintering thunder of bullets, reached a blazing crescendo, and then withered – only to be repeated elsewhere across the slope.

"Keep firing! Don't give them a chance!" the American Captain leading the troops who had circumnavigated the foot of the knoll cajoled his men and urged them on. "Give the bastards hell!"

A Russian officer, wild-eyed and dazed by a glancing head wound, shot one of his own men by accident then collapsed to the ground, his face a bloody mask.

From the trench atop the crest SACEUR could see a tideline of Russian bodies that showed how close they had come to overwhelming the outpost. The wounded and dead lay in clusters where the fighting had been the most ferocious. Now they were being driven back by a relentless torrent of fire that no man could stand in the face of.

Across the valley the enemy were in slow, stubborn retreat. The Russian armored advance had been weakened, then blunted, then pushed back by the arrival of the Abrams. And now the Russian infantry, isolated from support and caught in a hellish crossfire, began to retreat down the slope.

The smoke saved the Russian troops from complete annihilation. They melted away behind the swirling haze, their scattered fire twitching the haze as they withdrew east. A dozen Russians under the command of a junior officer broke away to the south. Behind the confusion of multiple explosions, they began clambering towards the crest of the knoll. Ponting saw the enemy soldiers and shouted an alarm. He pulled his M4 to his shoulder and sighted on the officer.

The Russians were just two hundred yards down the incline, cunningly using the mangled debris of destroyed BMP-2s to mask their ascent. Ponting waited for the curtain of smoke to part and fired. His bullets ricocheted off the steel hull of a burning Russian troop carrier. The enemy officer looked up, startled, and caught a fleeting sight of Ponting above the line of sandbags. He shouted to an infantryman standing beside him and the enemy soldier fired with his AK-74.

Ponting jinked away and ducked, knowing the bullets were aimed at him. The sandbag to his right burst open, shredded to pieces.

"What's happening?" Sergeant Harley growled.

"About a dozen enemy bastards off to the south. They're coming on fast," Ponting said in a gasp. His eyes were crazed with the closeness of death, his voice shaky.

Sergeant Harley slapped a fresh magazine into his M4 with the palm of his hand and stepped up onto the fire step. He scanned the smoke and grunted. "I see the fuckers," he snarled, then remembered SACEUR was standing in the trench nearby and muttered, "beggin' your pardon, sir."

SACEUR did not acknowledge the big Sergeant's apology. He was staring down at the half-buried body of an American soldier, his bullet-riddled corpse covered beneath a section of collapsed trench. The dead soldier's eyes were open, his glassy-eyed expression one of utter disbelief. He had been shot in the neck and chest, the blood from the gaping wounds now spattered like dry paint and crawling with flies.

Sergeant Harley watched two of the enemy soldiers down the slope break from their cover, running doubled over and diagonally across the ground towards a shell crater left from the Russian artillery bombardment. Harley sighted down the barrel of the M4 and opened fire. The lead Russian suddenly staggered, losing his stride. Then his legs went from underneath him and he fell face forward into the long grass. The second enemy soldier saw his comrade fall and fired wildly up the slope, screaming as he tried vainly to reach the cover of the crater. Sergeant Harley swung the barrel of the M4 onto the man and saw him jerk in spasms. The Russian dropped his weapon and fell, throwing his arms into the air as the bullets thwacked meatily into his torso. When he hit the ground, he was dead and splashed in blood. His lifeless body rolled down the slope and out of sight. A third Russian, fearful and disoriented, emerged from the veil of smoke calling out in confusion for his comrades. He blundered into the open and Harley shot the man in the neck. The Russian dropped to his knees vomiting blood, a rasping ragged sob in his throat.

The remaining Russians fired back at the crest. Their sudden burst of fire in the eerie aftermath of the infantry engagement further north attracted the attention of an alert American Lieutenant who turned his men onto the defiant Russians and cut them down with a hail of withering fire from the Platoon SAWs. Ponting waited until the hammering thunder of machine guns was just an echo and then cautiously raised his head above the blood-soaked rim of the trench.

Eight of the Russians were dead and two more were writhing in agony on the ground. Neither of the wounded Russians would live to see the new day.

SACEUR rose from the depths of the trench and surveyed the battlefield. Everywhere he looked the massed Russian attack was in retreat. Down on the valley's floor, a handful of T-72s were fighting a valiant rear-guard action while beyond them the remaining T-90s and BMP-2s whose crews had begun the afternoon with dreams of glory and triumph, retreated in abject defeat.

The Russian infantry that survived the fusillade from the two Companies of Americans were scrambling up the northern slope of the valley, making for the road that ran all the way back to the Lithuanian border. Some of the enemy troops were limping, others were being dragged or carried by their comrades. SACEUR let them go and instead scanned the far skyline where the valley opened onto far away farm fields. The smoke-smudged horizon was clear.

The Russian attack had failed, leaving the valley hazed with black smoke above a graveyard of dead men and destroyed armor.

The air reeked of blood, and the cloying, wafting stench of hundreds of corpses beginning to rot under the afternoon sun.

*

Lieutenant Colonel Chuck McCluskey caught sight of Guy Ponting out of the corner of his eye and called him over. The Colonel was locked in an intense conversation with SACEUR. The two senior officers parted and turned their attention to the exhausted young Lieutenant. Ponting's uniform was soaked in sweat and blood, his face so dark with streaks of grime that only his teeth and eyes showed white in the gruesome mask. He moved like a man twice his age, bone weary and still numbed with the shock of all he had experienced and witnessed.

Behind them the sky above Fort Suicide's LZ was encircled by Black Hawk helicopters, hovering in the air and waiting for their turn to unload supplies and recover the dead and injured. The clatter of their rotors turned the COP's shell-torn ground into a windswept wasteland, forcing the Battalion commander to raise his voice to a shout in order to be heard.

"The Company has been pretty badly beaten up," McCluskey explained. "Probably down to less than half strength. Captain Gatfield is dead and so is his XO."

"I'm sorry to hear that, sir," Ponting said dutifully, his voice scrubbed of all emotion. He wasn't sorry at all.

"So, I'm looking at you, Lieutenant Ponting, to assume the role of acting Company Commander – at least until the unit can be brought back up to strength. Do you want the job?"

Ponting looked away, back across the battlefield that was still shrouded in drifting smoke. The sun hung low in the sky, beginning to cast long shadows across the bodies of the dead. Behind him, the men of his Platoon were being led to a Black Hawk by Sergeant Harley. The men moved in shuffling, numbed steps, their bodies heavy with fatigue, but their shoulders straight.

"Thank you, sir," Ponting acknowledged the offer, then shook his head. "But I think I'd rather remain with my Platoon. You should find someone else for the job. These are my men, and we've experienced something here that has bound us together and will make us an even better fighting force in the months to come. I don't want to jeopardise that…"

Guy Ponting saluted formally, then strode towards the waiting Black Hawk. At the open cargo door he stopped and turned one last time, surveying the battlefield as if to sear the image into his memory. He would be back here in a week's time, after the Platoon had been rested and reinforced with fresh troops, after the bunkers and watchtower were rebuilt. But it would never be quite the same again. He felt he owed it to the memory of the men that died defending this patch of high ground to honor them all with a moment of profound gratitude. He took off his helmet, wiped the grime from his brow and bowed his head in solemn silence. One by one the men from the Platoon climbed back down from the Black Hawk and joined their Lieutenant in a ragged line of remembrance.

It was the very least the valiant dead deserved.

Epilogue:

Lieutenant Guy Ponting stared at himself in the fly-spotted mirror and reached for his razor. In the month since the battle the face that looked back had turned serious, the skin had sun-darkened, the mouth had curved down at the corners and become parenthesised by fine lines. He picked up the razor and lathered his jaw with soap, then scraped the blade across his cheek, leaving the skin smooth and brown in its wake.

The sudden clatter of an approaching helicopter carried on the breeze. Beyond the sandbagged wall of the bunker, he sensed men moving towards the LZ to greet the new arrivals. He kept shaving, his ears following the sound of the Black Hawk as it hovered and then sank down the sky to land.

A few moments later the Black Hawk lifted off again and as the sound faded, the voice of Sergeant Harley carried clear across the compound.

"Welcome to Combat Outpost Bravo Zero-Six," Ponting heard him addressing the three new arrivals from Warsaw that would bring his Platoon back up to full strength. "Around here we call the place 'Heroes Hill' because every damned man in this Platoon has earned the honor. You're lucky. You're joining an elite unit of veterans, led by a veteran Lieutenant."

Ponting's eyebrows arched in sudden curious surprise at his Sergeant's overheard comment. He frowned, then wiped the soap from his face and peered more closely at his reflection. He saw it then; the dark shadows of memories stirring behind his unblinking eyes, the new web of fine facial lines, and the intangible set to his jaw that was indelibly different to how he remembered himself when he had first arrived at the battlefront.

He realised then that he had become what every soldier aspired to be.

Just a few short days in the fiery forge of conflict had tempered and hardened him like steel, and given him the calm self-assurance that other men were drawn to and would willingly follow.

Guy Ponting was a combat veteran.

Facebook: https://www.facebook.com/NickRyanWW3
Website: https://www.worldwar3timeline.com

Author's note:
For the sake of the story, I have given the little Polish locations of Szelment and Postawelek more substance as villages than their geographic imagery suggests. In reality, both locations consist of just a couple of grouped buildings.

Acknowledgements:
The greatest thrill of writing, for me, is the opportunity to research the subject matter and to work with military, political and historical experts from around the world. I had a lot of help researching this book from the following groups and people. I am forever grateful for their willing enthusiasm and cooperation. Any remaining technical errors are mine.

Jill Blasy:
Jill has the editorial eye of an eagle! I trust Jill to read every manuscript, picking up typographical errors, missing commas, and for her general 'sense' of the book. Jill has been a great friend and a valuable part of my team for several years.

Jan Wade:
Jan is my Personal Assistant and an indispensable part of my team. She is a thoughtful, thorough, professional and persistent pleasure to work with. Chances are, if you're reading this book, it's due to Jan's engaging marketing and promotional efforts.

Samael Garcia:
Sam was a Black Hawk helicopter pilot in the US Army and is now a commercial airline pilot. He has been making me look smarter than I really am since I was writing military zombie fiction.

Dale Simpson:
Dale is a retired Special Forces operator who has been helping me with the military aspects of my writing since I first put pen to paper. He is my first point of contact for military

technical advice. Over the years that he has been saving me from stupid mistakes we've become firm friends. The authenticity of the action and combat sequences in this novel are due to Dale's diligence and willing cooperation.

The Queen's Royal Hussars:

My thanks to the social media people at the British Army who were kind enough to clarify some organizational details of 'The Devil's Children' tank squadron.

Dave Hamlyn-Wright:

Englishman, Dave Hamlyn-Wright, is one of the world's foremost authorities on military vehicles. He is also the owner of the http://tanknutdave.com website. Dave checked through the details of the clash between the British Challenger 2 tanks and the Russian T-90s to ensure the information was technically accurate and realistic.

Dion Walker Sr:

Sergeant First Class (Retired) Dion Walker Sr, served 21 proud years in the US Army with deployments during Operation Desert Shield/Storm, Operation Intrinsic Action and Operation Iraqi Freedom. For 17 years he was a tanker in several Armor Battalions and Cavalry Squadrons before spending 4 years as an MGS (Stryker Mobile Gun System) Platoon Sergeant in a Stryker Infantry Company.

Dion was a tremendous help in verifying important technical and tactical details once the first draft of the manuscript was complete.

Printed in Great Britain
by Amazon